Mr. Fred L. Fowl[illegible]
18 Armstrong
Hillsdale, Mich.

Merritt Green

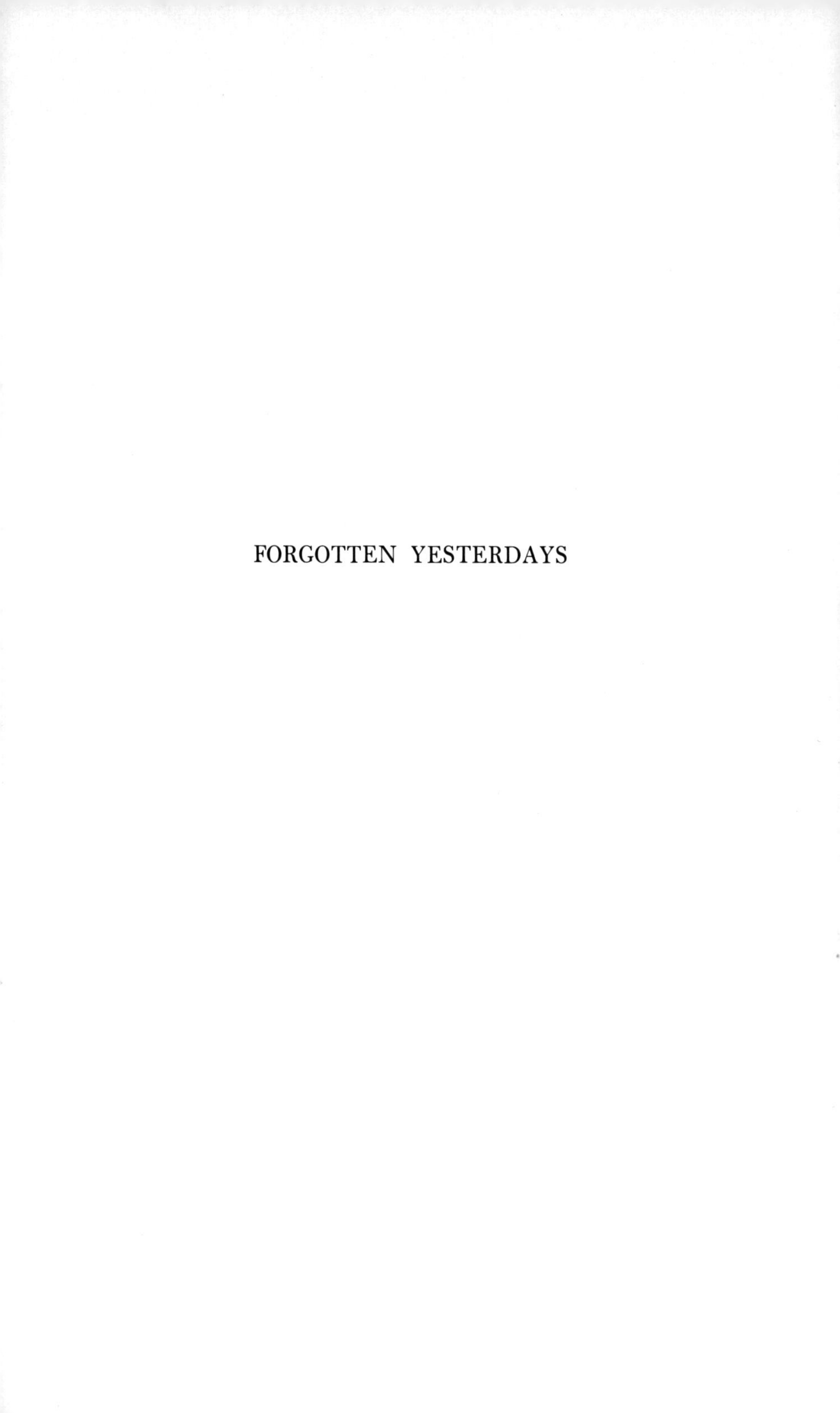

FORGOTTEN YESTERDAYS

FORGOTTEN YESTERDAYS

A Tale of Early Michigan

by
MERRITT GREENE

Chapter Head Drawings
by
JANE PENFOLD

HILLSDALE SCHOOL SUPPLY, INC., *Publishers*
Hillsdale, Michigan
1964

With the exception of actual historical personages identified as such, the characters are entirely the product of the author's imagination and have nothing but a coincidental resemblance to any person in real life.

Library of Congress Card Number 64-17629

Printed in the United States of America

TO

MY GRANDCHILDREN

Daniel, Geoffrey and Jennifer Greene

and

Jayne Greene Kampe

When the hill of toil was steepest,
When the forest frown was deepest,
    Poor, but young, you hastened here;
Came, where solid hope was cheapest —
    Came — a pioneer.
Made the western jungles view
    Civilization's charms;
Snatched a home for yours and you,
    From the lean tree arms.
Toil had never cause to doubt you —
    Progress' path you helped to clear;
But today forgets about you,
And the world rides on without you —
    Sleep, old pioneer!

From "Sleep Old Pioneer"
By Will Carleton.

CONTENTS

1

When The Council Fire Burned Low

THE great council fire of the assembled Huron-Potowatomi west of Allen's Prairie had dwindled to embers on that June night in 1838. The main chiefs and the sub-chiefs had wrapped themselves in their blankets for the night, and finally Pamasaw and his white friend, Martin Langdon were alone.

"Now," said Pamasaw, "we can talk. I need your advice."

"Advice is cheap, Pamasaw. It's all I can afford to give away at the present time. I'm just a beginning homesteader, you know."

Martin packed some tobacco from his pouch, into his pipe.

"You live rent free on land my father gave you—you and Owaysa. Are you happy with her, Martin?"

Martin thoughtfully placed an ember from the dying fire into the bowl of his pipe. "I ought to be. I've the prettiest wife in the state of Michigan – some of the best land on earth. My wife loves me. I have enough to eat, and we only lack some children."

"You have not said whether or not you are happy."

"Why do you ask?"

"Because, Martin, you are married. I am not. I have seen twenty-six winters. I'm old to be without a wife. You have Owaysa, but I have only a longing in my heart. The girl I love is the daughter of Chief Moquago."

"But you're the son of Chief Baw Beese. You have the right to ask her."

"I already have."

"She doesn't love you?"

"She says we must wait. I've waited ever since I first saw her at the meeting of the tribes in Chicago. That was five years ago."

"That's too long to wait for any girl." Martin puffed on his pipe.

"Wenojah's her name." Pamasaw began drawing designs with a stick around the dying fire. "It means meadowlark. Her voice is beautiful, and she is very lovely. I want no other. But she hates palefaces."

"Well and good. So she wants no part of white people. You could leave her at home when you go to the settlements."

"It's not that simple, Martin, She says we must wait until the palefaces are no longer among us."

"She must be blind to what's happening around her. You and I will never live to see that day, Pamasaw."

"But she insists it must be that way — or she will not marry."

"Then you'd better forget her, and find yourself another girl for a wife."

"But just any girl won't do. Listen, Martin, when an Indian boy becomes of age he goes into the forest and waits to commune with his manitou. When my manitou came I was told that I would marry a girl a distance from our village — a great man's daughter. I must be true to my manitou."

"Perhaps Wenojah doesn't love you."

"She's accepted some of my gifts. I gave her a beautiful deerskin, tanned white, which she made into a skirt and jacket. But once when I gave her some blue cloth I bought in Grannisville, she refused it — because it had been made by the Ke-moke-mon."

"If you're true to your manitou and she's true to her vow, Pamasaw, you're going to be a bachelor."

"Perhaps, after tomorrow, when she learns that we sell no more land, she will change her mind."

"There may be other daughters of great men who live at a distance from Ko-jess-sug-wa-seepe."

Pamasaw sighed. "But there is only one Wenojah?"

Martin gazed into the fire, puffing thoughtfully on his pipe. Once he had felt like that about Owaysa, only there had been a girl named Ellen Van Duzer. She had convinced him for a time that she was to marry him — although really he never quite believed it, and now he realized it was always Owaysa. Unknowingly he was seeking Owaysa when he left New York state to pioneer in Michigan Territory. It was some sort of destiny that had drawn them together in the wilderness — Owaysa, the half-breed daughter of Osseo and a white mother. She pretended she hated him at first, because he was white. Now she admitted she too had loved him from the day they had met.

But having a half-breed wife did some strange things occasionally — such as involving him in this present trip to Branch with Chief Baw Beese, the head of the tribe of which Owaysa had been — still considered herself — a member.

"Tell me, Pamasaw," Martin said. "Just what was it that was said before the council fire tonight, when the flames were high and the chiefs were talking?"

"I forget," said Pamasaw, "that while I learned English of you — and though you are married to Owaysa, you still don't speak our language."

"There was that big butcher knife that an Indian presented your father. Why was that, Pamasaw?"

"That, Martin, was introduced as the law of the knife."

"What's that?"

"Any Indian or sub-chief who goes against the wishes of the assembled council will be killed with that knife."

"I see. Such as what wish, Pamasaw?"

"Selling more land to the Ke-moke-mon."

Martin was silent for a minute and knocked the ashes from his pipe, then inquired, "Would anyone be likely to do that?"

"I hope not, but Sau-en-quett was pretty surly about it."

"Who's he?"

"Sau-en-quett is a sub-chief under Moquago. He lives on the reservation called Mickesaube, or Happy Waters. The white people already have two villages on the edges of it — called Lyons and Masonville. Then there's another place called Branch to the south of it. That's where the meeting with the government agent takes place tomorrow."

"I don't like the sound of it, Pamasaw. And I don't know why I should leave my farm work to come to a meeting with government agents. The last time I did that I got in trouble. Remember?"

"Yes, I remember. But this is different. Besides, my father gave you the land you and Owaysa live on. You owe it to him to help tomorrow. You can explain what the Indians want. We can't. The government agent will listen to you."

"I like your confidence. But I don't like getting in trouble. If somebody gets killed I don't want to be involved in it."

"That's what we're hoping will be prevented, by this council fire tonight. You noticed we were met by Moquago's band and that we're west of Allen's Prairie?"

"And then we came deep into the woods. I never saw so many Indians in this part of the country before."

* * * * *

"And then Moquago rose up, when the council fire was at its highest, and he said: "The paleface farmer is among us. He plows our land. It is futile for us to close our eyes and hope he will go away. He is here, but what can we do about it?"

And as Martin listened to the tale as told by Pamasaw, it was as though the assemblage was convening and speaking Indian although it was translated into English.

When Moquago had concluded, the Indian named Sau-en-quett — the crafty Sau-en-quett, with a scar on his face, giving him the appearance of a perpetual sneer, rose next.

"Sell him the land," said Sau-en-quett. "Move deeper into the forest. The Long Knives know they can take the land anyhow. The sound of the ax and the sawmill is among us. Whenever he wants to the paleface says: 'Injun, move over,' and we move. Now he wants Happy Waters. Me and my little band will sell it to him."

Chief Baw Beese next arose with great dignity, and said firmly: "You are a fool, Sau-en-quett. You talk like a fool, and you counsel like a fool."

Martin saw Sau-en-quett finger the hatchet at his waist, and his face with the sneer changed to a sinister look of hate.

"Chief Baw Beese, you are getting old," said Sau-en-quett, not taking his hand away from his hatchet. "I shall not be called a fool! I ask all chiefs who agree with me, to join me at that cedar tree."

Sau-en-quett turned lightly on his feet, and walked to a juniper that stood close by. But neither chiefs nor braves joined him.

"It is I who am right." Baw Beese smiled. "You ignore the councils of others. Both the councils of Moquago and my own have decided the same."

"To sell no more land to the United States!" Sau-en-quett's scar deepened into more of a sneer than usual. "Is that what this council fire is for? Just to tell us that we have no more to say about it than a deer we're about to kill?"

"Brothers! Cousins!" Chief Baw Beese addressed the assemblage. "You've heard Sau-en-quett advise us to sell our birthright to the Long Knives. Our two bands, which came westward from Detroit together, after we signed a treaty with the United States giving up our holdings on the Huron and Raisin rivers are united.* In return for this we receive four hundred dollars a year and live at peace with the Long Knives as they come. But we are still a part of the great United Nation — the Three Council Fires — of Potowatomi, Chippewa and Ottawa. Our councils have individually voted against selling more land."

"I ask you to consider the wishes of our council. Without a treaty they cannot move us to the land of the setting sun as they have very definitely planned on doing. They will say: 'The land is gone. We have no place for you but across the Mississippi'."

Chief Baw Beese looked around the circle by the council fire, drew his blanket around him and sat down.

Pamasaw and other young men replenished the fuel, and the blaze, re-kindled, lighted the dark faces with a ruddy glow, seeming to catch the fleeting colors of the sunset as the twilight deepened into night.

Chief Moquago arose majestically from his seat at the forefront of his band, and addressed the group in commanding tones. Martin drew closer to Pamasaw, who continued translating what was said.

"Our cousin, Baw Beese, speaks well. Our band has decided to sell no more land to the Ke-moke-mon! I do not know what some of the other sub-chiefs like Sau-en-quett have decided around their own council fires, but at the council fires of Nottawa-Seepe we have voted. So now let this entire assemblage of chiefs and braves vote as his spirit and his manitou guides him to do. As the majority votes, so vote I, Moquago, a main chief of the Huron-Potowatomi. Let all who are in favor of selling the rest of our lands to the Ke-moke-mon tomorrow, rise and say so."

Only Sau-en-quett came forward. "Though I am all alone I shall sell the site of Happy Waters to the Long Knives."

* NOTE: The chief refers to the treaties of 1805 and 1807 signed by the two bands in Detroit.

"Choo-ween! Choo-ween!" was grunted in disapproval around the camp fire.

"Then all of you who are against selling our land to the Ke-moke-mon, rise and make your statement." Moquago had barely finished his request when the entire assemblage rose shouting to its feet, rending the forest with the loud yells of "Choo-ween! Choo-ween!"

"Aowh!" came the lone voice of Sau-en-quett, who then sat sullenly aloof by his juniper tree. The others resumed their places around the council fire, and only Moquago remained standing.

Martin saw a couple of Indians conferring in an undertone.

Then the more handsome of the two arose, holding a shining knife such as the pioneers termed a butcher knife. He approached Moquago with the knife.

"What are you doing with that knife, Kakatoma?" Moquago demanded.

"Cush-a-wees says he presents this knife to be used on a chief, sub-chief, or brave, who disobeys the edict of this council."

"A-owh! A-owh!" shouted the seated Indians.

Kakatoma offered the knife, handle first to Chief Moquago, who accepted it, and presented it to Baw Beese.

"We accept this knife from Cush-a-wees," Moquago said gravely, "and give it into the keeping of our cousin."

Chief Baw Beese rose, and the flames reflected blood red on the shining blade. "Is it agreed then that we have the law of the knife for tomorrow?"

"Aowh!" A-owh!" shouted all but one.

"Choo-ween!" said Sau-en-quett.

"Well, Sau-en-quett, you alone vote differently than all others," said Baw Beese. "You say yes when all of us say no, and you say no when all of us say yes. Why do you do this?"

Sau-en-quett's sneer of derision could not have been greater had he tried for days to achieve his disdainful superiority.

"You are indeed being silly children," said Sau-en-quett. "If the Long Knives offer us anything at all for the land we should take it. There are so many of them they could take it away from us and give us nothing. I am not foolish, my brothers. The foolish ones are yourselves. As to this law of the knife, I have grave doubts as to who might wield it."

"The knife will be used if any disobey the edicts of this council," said Chief Moquago. "There will be no land sold to the Ke-moke-mon."

"The Long Knives already have divided this land into Hillsdale and Branch counties, and that is all the land we can claim. And already, Moquago, you signed a treaty in Chicago in 1833 . . . ."

"No! No!" Moquago thundered, his brow clouding in fury. "My mark was made while my hand was held by a drunken man! Were you the one who guided my hand, Sau-en-quett? I was so beaten that blood was in my eyes and I could not see you. Were you the one?"

The old chief took the knife from Baw Beese, and held it aloft in the air. "I invoke the manitous of the forest to hear me!" said Chief Moquago. "The law of the knife on this council fire shall be upheld. I swear it by the bones of my grandfather!"

An anachronism of the tribal council was born out at that moment by the distant squeal of a settler's pig, and the mooing of a cow.

But none of the assembly paid heed to the invasion of the ancient sounds of the forest. Even Sau-en-quett was slightly awed, as he answered, "It was not I, Moquago." He eyed the glittering knife as he stepped back. "It was a member of the Pokagon band, under the guidance of Topinabee."

"Ugh!" Moquago grunted, and sat down staring morosely into the council fire.

The mystic circle vanished as the men sought their tents, or lay on the open ground. Only Martin and Pamasaw sat silently together.

Suddenly, Martin realized his friend had been right. The conduct of Sau-en-quett would certainly bear watching when the group convened at Branch on the morrow.

"And my only hope," Pamasaw said, "is that Wenojah, the Meadowlark, will be reasonable and see that the Long Knives will not go away."

"Yes," said Martin. "Let us hope she will."

But while Pamasaw thought more of his beloved than of the outcome of the morrow, Martin only visualized the knife as it shimmered in the fire — and the sneer on the scarred face of Sau-en-quett.

2

Choo-ween! Choo-ween! And A-owh! A-owh!

A hazy sun showed through the morning mists — a big red disk, like a shield stained with blood — as the dusky denizens of the forest girded themselves for the remainder of their journey, and their pow-wow with the representative of the Great White Father in Washington.

Many were resplendent in silver bracelets, with feathers in their hair — the best style of backwoods finery. Chief Baw Beese and Chief Moquago together with the sub-chiefs were magnificent in their full panoply of beaded buckskins. The younger braves, like Pama-saw, were naked to the waist, content merely with painting their faces in various hues, and wearing silver ornaments on their arms and necks.

Sau-en-quett, aping the custom of the two main chiefs, was garbed in ornamental buckskins, plus added feathers in his hair; while Cush-a-wees and Kakatoma, more modest in their dress, grumbled at the fine airs Sau-en-quett assumed as he strutted about prepara-tory to breaking camp.

The word was spoken at last by Baw Beese and Moquago, and the cortege followed the two main chiefs back to the Chicago road, where they headed west for a few miles, then turning southward in the forest to the place known as Branch.*

The settlement of Branch, which the founders hoped to make the county seat of Branch county, was composed of a tavern, a black-smith shop, and a log dwelling. There was a small clearing around the buildings, and some pretext of streets being laid out.

*NOTE: The actual scene of this rendezvous was in Mendon, but as subsequent activities were centered in Coldwater, and the events all concerned Coldwater, we have seen fit to have the meeting in the settlement known as Branch.

The Indians halted at the edge of the clearing, and awaited a sign from the tavern. A small table and several barrels stood near the doorway of the building.

Presently, coming through the doorway of the tavern and into the clearing was a man of medium stature and indeterminate age, wearing a tall hat, a plum-colored coat, high collar, frilled shirt, and fawn-colored breeches, which marked him either as a gentleman or a dandy. As he carried a gold-headed cane, Martin concluded he was probably a gentleman. The Indians looked curiously at the man, but murmured in dissatisfaction as there emerged from the tavern door a squad of blue-coated soldiers, with pistols in their belts and drawn swords, as though they were anticipating trouble.

Martin noticed several Indians reaching for their knives and tomahawks when Chief Baw Beese commanded: "Choo Ween! Choo Ween!"

But the Indians' dark eyes looked with suspicion at the young soldiers.

Chief Baw Beese, addressing the man in the tall hat, inquired: "Why do Long Knives come with drawn swords, when ask for peace talk?"

"Just to show you, Chief whatever your name is, that we mean business this time."

"Ugh!" The chief frowned, and grunted. His frown and his grunt were echoed by all the young braves, the sub-chiefs and by Chief Moquago.

"For why you think we come if we not think you mean talk business?" Moquago asked. "Great White Father sent word, meet agent here. We come, but we got knives too. Mebbe not long like yours, but knives."

"Now my man don't get insolent!" The man in the tall hat thumped his gold-headed cane pompously on the ground. "We're only protecting ourselves. Should there be trouble we have an entire company of cavalry awaiting our command."

Martin realized that the government agent was bluffing, and so did the Indians, for there was a general movement toward the little squad of soldiers, and looks of savage ferocity were about to give forth to a war whoop, when chief Baw Beese said, "Martin, you talk quick!"

"Just a minute," said Martin, stepping forward. "Let me have a few words with you before you seek to continue your parley, Mr. . . ."

"Name's Butler — Josiah Butler!" said the government agent in astonishment. "You white or half Indian?"

"I'll introduce myself — Langdon. Martin Langdon, now of Hillsdale county, state of Michigan; but formerly from Erie county, New York. I'm a white man!"

Martin extended his hand, and Butler grasped it gingerly, and asked, "Can you get some sense into the skulls of these savages?"

"Sense, Mr. Butler, has to work both ways out here. You're trying to get a treaty signed, I believe."

"That's right. The government wants an end to this claim on land these Indians have, and an end to the reservation called Mick-e-sawbe,* through which the Chicago Turnpike passes."

"These Indians are ordinarily peacable. I've lived here for the past six years, and I ought to know."

"I've heard differently in Washington! A man named Derbyshire who used to be assistant to Governor Porter says they're dangerous. And a settler named Maxon has written they're troublesome. He lives in Hillsdale county, by the way."

"Derbyshire is not too reliable, and as to Maxon, he's a newcomer. I don't know him."

Butler leaned on his gold-headed cane and looked narrowly at Martin. The Indians looked apprehensively at the blue-coated cavalrymen, and mumbled among themselves.

"I advise you, Mr. Butler, to have that squad of soldiers sheath their swords," Martin continued. "Nobody believes you when you say you have a small army in hiding. The Indians have you all accounted for, be very sure of that."

Butler cast a furtive look about him. "But would we be safe if they sheath their swords?"

"Make no show of force, Mr. Butler. You'd best send your bodyguard back into the tavern."

"Suppose they attack?"

"After all, Mr. Butler, I hope you don't think a squad of soldiers could protect you against all these Indians. If you've a proposition to make, get on with it. But just get those men to put away their swords."

* NOTE: Mick-e-sawbe formed the downtown portion of the present city of Coldwater.

It was with apparent misgiving that Butler acquiesced. Turning, he said, "Corporal Webb, sheath the sabers and retire."

When the corporal gave the command, and the soldiers had returned to the tavern, the assembled Indians relaxed. But Butler looked with apprehension and turning to Martin, said, "That makes you and I the only white men out here."

"I know, but they've come peaceably. Just keep it on that basis—if you can."

The Indians began arranging themselves in a semi-circle with the main chiefs in the forefront. Martin started to walk away to join Pamasaw.

"Wait!" shouted Butler, his pompous dignity obviously ruffled. "I'll need you to interpret, Langdon!"

"I'm not bilingual, Mr. Butler. I know only a few words. If you need an interpreter my friend, Pamasaw, speaks both English and Potowatomi. I taught him the English."

"Summon him, please," Butler commanded.

Pamasaw came forward reluctantly without waiting for Martin to call him. "I'll translate your message for you," he said, looking Butler in the eye.

Butler seemed dubious, but said, "Very well, then I want you to stand on one side of me, and Langdon on the other. I'll feel safer that way."

Pamasaw said, "Will what you have to say make my brothers angry?"

Butler cleared his throat, and said "No, of course not. Or rather, I hope not. But I want you to translate my words accurately."

"It shall be as you say," Martin said. "Pamasaw is a good and fluent interpreter."

"The Great White Father in Washington," began Butler, "has asked me to explain that it is no longer desirable for us to have no treaties with the small tribe of Huron-Potowatomi. So far as can be ascertained the United States has treaties signed by such chiefs as Topinabee, Pokagon and others giving title to all this land, yet there seems to be territory comprising Hillsdale and Branch counties which you claim for some reason known only to yourselves, has never been deeded to the United States of America."

When Pamasaw translated Mr. Butler's preliminary statement there was only silence among the Indians. It was at that time that

Martin observed some of the older Indian women lurking on the fringes of the clearing around the tavern.

"It is no longer desirable," Mr. Butler continued, "for your reservation of Mick-e-sawbe to occupy its present site on the Chicago Turnpike. It frightens emigrants, and delays the building of the little village of Coldwater.* That is why I have chosen to address you at Branch instead of either Lyons or Masonville. I don't wish to address you on what you deem your own special reservation, although I have been informed in Washington by a man named Derbyshire, who was familiar with this territory, that the land there all belongs to a chief named Sau-en-quett. Perhaps I should deal with Sau-en-quett alone."

Cries of "Choo-ween! Choo-ween!" greeted this portion of the speech as soon as Pamasaw had rendered the translation.

"What's the meaning of 'Choo-ween'?" the government agent asked.

"It means No! Emphatically no!" Martin said.

Butler hesitated for a moment and then continued along a different line. "The United States," he said, "will give you, in exchange for the signing of a treaty on all lands in Hillsdale and Branch counties, an equal amount of land west of the Mississippi river in Iowa territory. Besides that we will give you much whiskey and pails of pretty pieces of silver."

Although Butler beamed pleasantly as he explained the large-hearted generosity of the United States government, the menacing chorus echoed again through the forests, "Choo-ween! Choo-ween!"

Moquago came majestically forward, and addressed Butler in the loud, clear tones of the Indian orator.

"The Huron-Potowatomi have one treaty, separate from all others with the Long Knives," he said in his native tongue. "We ceded land around Detroit in the time of our fathers and grandfathers, and before the great chief Tecumseh called the children of the forest together on the warpath. But this treaty says we are to be paid four hundred dollars a year forever for our lands on the Huron and Raisin rivers. We ceded this land to the Long Knives and moved west of a line running north from Fort Defiance to the Grand River at Jacksonburg. We want nothing more from the Long Knives except

*NOTE: The Chicago Turnpike, now U.S. 12, ran through the middle of the reservation on the present site of Coldwater.

to be left alone. We are only interested in freedom from interference in our affairs."

Pamasaw dutifully translated the speech of Moquago, and Butler's face at first turned pale in disbelief. He clutched at the top of his gold-headed cane with one hand, and his other hand was clenched in anger. But he refrained from speaking until his anger had subsided.

"But I offer you many pails of silver and barrels and barrels of good whiskey. Besides there's all that beautiful land on the plains west of the Mississippi where there are no palefaces — no Long Knives, as you choose to call us."

When Pamasaw had translated this, Chief Moquago's brow knitted stubbornly, and he said: "There will be the Sioux, the Omaha, and others like them who are our mortal enemies. We should then have to call on the Long Knives to protect us from our enemies, and that would not be good. We want freedom from the Long Knives and not have to call on them for help — not any more of it. You will please to keep the treaties you have made with our people, and we will make no trouble. If you would help us at all send us the teachers and the blacksmiths you have already promised us, and pay them so they will stay with us."

Mr. Butler was no longer angry. For the moment he was nonplussed when he heard the translation of Moquago's speech, and the chief made his way back to the semi-circle of Indians. Then the government agent turned to Martin and asked: "What does he mean about not paying teachers and blacksmiths? Is there anything to that nonsense?"

"I once taught in Grannisville," said Martin. "There was so much difficulty over the pay that I quit, and became a settler. As for blacksmiths there never were any."

It was while Butler was deliberating Martin's statement that Sau-en-quett burst from the circle of Indians, and inquired of the government agent: "How much whiskey do we get?"

Butler immediately brightened up, and drawing a large legal-looking document from his coat-tail, laid it on the table, smiling. "My man," he said, "You'll get all the whiskey in these barrels here on the ground if you sign this treaty."

Sau-en-quett was joined by a pretty little woman as he went to the table and bent over the official paper.

"My husband, he can read — half French," she said proudly.

After reading the entire document Sau-en-quett turned to the assembled Indians and began a passionate harrangue which Martin assumed was urging them to sign the treaty. This was even more evident as Pamasaw frowned questioningly from time to time, and made no effort to translate to either Butler or to Martin.

It was Pamasaw himself who led, at the end of Sau-en-quett's impassioned plea, "Choo-ween!" And all the assembled Indians joined in shouting the inevitable words, "Choo-ween!"

"So!" said Sau-en-quett angrily in English. "It's 'no,' is it?" He faced Butler, and said with dignity. "I can see, Mr. Butler, it's only a matter of time, and you'll get what you want, anyhow! Give me the pen! I will sign!"

Butler handed Sau-en-quett the quill pen, which he then dipped into an ink well on the table.

"Can you write, too?" Butler inquired.

"I can write, but I'll make my mark as well." Sau-en-quett was scornful as he started scratching on the document.

"Choo-ween! Choo-ween!" cried the assembled Indians, and Chief Baw Beese stepped forward protesting the action. The chief grasped the hand of Sau-en-quett and a great blot appeared on the paper. Sau-en-quett turning, cried: "Wunna-Moshe!" and shoved the chief so hard he fell backwards and was caught by Pamasaw, who quickly reached for his tomahawk.

But Baw Beese said quietly, "Choo-ween!"

The scar on Sau-en-quett's face seemed to increase in size as he hurriedly and boldly finished signing the document.

"Remember the knife! The law of the knife!" muttered Pamasaw.

It was uttered only in an undertone, but Martin could see that Sau-en-quett had heard it, and for a brief moment the scar on his face did not reflect the customary sneer.

"Listen you!" Sau-en-quett said, drawing himself up to his full height. "I've sold only what I have a right to sell — I've sold Mick-sawbe, and I'd sell it again for two quarts of whiskey!"

He turned to Butler, and handing him the pen, said, "Now you sign to make it binding. The rest will not sign. I've ceded you Mick-e-sawbe!"

Butler signed the document, as the assembled Indians looked on. Martin expected an outburst at any moment, but for some reason he could not understand, the silence was more ominous.

Sau-en-quett looked defiantly at the main chiefs, the other sub-chiefs and braves. Only his little wife looked at him in worshipful admiration.

"Whiskey now," demanded Sau-en-quett.

"It's in the barrels," said Butler. "I'll have to open a barrel. Wouldn't it be better to wait until these others have gone?"

Sau-en-quett's back was turned to the Indians and he looked closely at the barrels of whiskey. He was not aware, as was Martin, that Cush-a-wees was approaching him rapidly, brandishing his tomahawk. Butler looked up as Cush-a-wees was raising the tomahawk high over the head of Sau-en-quett, then he fell back, mortally wounded. The little wife of Sau-en-quett was smiling and holding in her hand a green-handled knife she had thrust into the heart of Cush-a-wees. It was all so sudden, that nobody actually saw it happen, but as Cush-a-wees fell, there was general vocal animosity in the undertones from the Indians, and Sau-en-quett, who saw what had happened, holding his wife by the waist, faced them all, and spoke in Potowatomi, pointing at the whiskey barrels, with a look of smirking triumph.

But the Indians did not accept the invitation to the firewater. "I don't understand it," said Butler. "It's contrary to Indian nature. What's the reason they killed this Indian just now?"

"Because he was going to kill Sau-en-quett," Martin explained.

As with one voice, the Indians yelled, and began converging on Sau-en-quett, who, seeing their temper, whirled and fled into the tavern with his wife.

As the Indians reached Butler and Martin, Baw Beese was in the forefront. "You've bought Mick-e-sawbe," said the chief. "Sau-en-quett sold it to you, against vote of tribe. But we honor. We give you Mick-e-sawbe! But we not take whiskey — not now!"

So saying the chief buried his tomahawk into one of the whiskey barrels, and the air was filled with the smell of cheap whiskey, heavily watered down, and colored with a quantity of tobacco. The Indians, Martin observed, looked sad to see so much good firewater flowing onto the ground, but since both Baw Beese and Moquago had been obdurate in not accepting government generosity none dared to intervene as Baw Beese whacked open another barrel.

Martin saw Moquago summon Kakatoma, handing over to him the long knife. Butler, turning to Martin, said, "This is all the whiskey the government sent. What shall I do?"

But Martin had no time to answer. He knew that so far as the government was concerned Sau-en-quett would be regarded as a good Indian. He must prevent, if possible, the death of the chief who had signed the treaty, for surely the Indians would be in serious trouble if anything happened to this treacherous sub-chief.

He was watching Kakatoma, and not listening to Butler. He must get that knife if possible, but Kakatoma was about to enter the tavern door when Warren the tavern-keeper burst out onto the scene.

"Stop them!" he yelled. "They'll be burning down the tavern next."

The Indians were wrecking the table on which Sau-en-quett had signed the document, but Martin was close on the heels of Kakatoma, as he entered the tavern door.

3

The Aftermath Of The Ceding Of Mick-e-sawbe

When Martin followed Kakatoma into the tavern, he saw Sau-en-quett standing alone at the bar. Nobody else was in the little room.

Sau-en-quett, resplendent in his finest regalia, demanded something of Kakatoma in the Potowatomi tongue.

Kakatoma, the long knife flashing in his hand, answered, and swung the blade in the air. Sau-en-quett pulled his hunting knife and stood defiantly, awaiting Kakatoma's attack.

"No, Kakatoma!" said Martin.

The Indians both looked at him.

"Law of knife!" said Kakatoma. But as he turned, Sau-en-quett took a step towards him, and would have closed on him. But Martin stepped between them, and smashing Kakatoma in the jaw, knocked him out of balance.

As Sau-en-quett paused at this turn of events, his wife entered the room.

"Chee-chee-qua!" said Sau-en-quett. "Get soldier here!"

"Choo-ween!" said Kakatoma.

But Chee-chee-qua, obeying her husband, went outside the tavern door.

"There's no law of the knife now!" Martin said, standing between the two Indians. "It'll be just plain murder, Kakatoma."

Kakatoma might have sprung on Martin, but the soldiers came into the small room with Chee-chee-qua, who pointed at Kakatoma.

"He try to keel husband," she said.

Corporal Webb stepped forward. "Give me that butcher knife!" he commanded.

"No!"

Kakatoma jerked away, and leaped out the back door of the tavern. Corporal Webb fired a shot from his pistol after the fleeing Indian, but the ball only lodged in the door casing.

"May need help," said Sau-en-quett. "They talk law of the knife!"

"Don't worry," said Corporal Webb. "We'll keep him from hurting you."

Martin was dubious about the protection to be afforded by a squad of soldiers unless they intended to stay indefinitely as a body-guard. Sau-en-quett, in the eyes of the Indians, had violated one of their own laws. Not even Chief Baw Beese would consider it a murder, but rather an execution.

"We stay with soldier," said Sau-en-quett to his wife.

"A-owh!" she smiled at her husband.

"Come, men, we'd better get back outside," said the corporal, and they went back to the front of the building, followed closely by Sau-en-quett and his wife. Martin was standing in the doorway when he caught a fleeting glimpse of Kakatoma, lost in the crowd of milling Indians.

The body of the dead Cush-a-wees was being carried away into the forest. The air was acrid with the smell of rotgut whiskey, and the Indians had made kindling of the table on which the treaty had been signed.

Butler stood looking at the document which gave Mick-e-sawbe to the United States of America.

"More whiskey!" demanded Sau-en-quett.

"There's no more now," said Butler sadly. "They ought to all be arrested for destroying government property."

"And mine!" said Warren. "What about my table? It's kindling!"

"Sold Mick-e-sawbe!" said Sau-en-quett. "Want whiskey!"

"But there isn't any left I tell you," said Butler.

"You promise!" said Sau-en-quett stubbornly.

Butler was becoming impatient. He turned to Elisha Warren.

"Take this Indian inside, Warren. Give him all the whiskey he wants!"

"But . . . ." Warren was apprehensive.

"The United States will pay for it."

Warren acquiesced with bad grace, saying, "I still think they all ought to be arrested and made to pay for my table."

Sau-en-quett followed Warren back into the tavern, but Chee-

chee-qua, whose name meant Robin in English, stood close to Butler.

"Arrest Kakatoma," she said. "Please! He keel my husband!"

"He seems very much alive to me."

"But he will keel. Please — please arrest!"

"What about it, Langdon? You seem to know everything about these Indians."

"He hasn't killed anybody yet, but he has the long knife."

"Could arrest him and hold him until we made them pay Warren for that table. A squad of men can't arrest a couple of hundred Indians."

"They won't pay for the table, Mr. Butler," said Martin.

"At least we can try it." He turned to the soldiers, and said: "Corporal Webb, arrest Kakatoma!"

"I can't tell one Indian from another," the corporal admitted. "Which is Kakatoma?"

"Me show," said Chee-chee-qua. "Me know where Kakatoma live!"

"Then show him," said Butler.

"To horse then," said the corporal.

"A-owh! Me get horse too," said Chee-chee-qua.

The bluecoats and the little Indian woman went behind the tavern where the horses were tied.

"She won't find Kakatoma," said Martin. "He has all outdoors to hide out in. And had you stopped to think that pretty little Indian woman is guilty of murder?"

"How you talk, Langdon!"

"You saw her stab Cush-a-wees, right before your eyes."

"Oh that! It was a proposition of self-defense, I say. He was going to tomahawk her husband — think of it, Langdon — that Cush-a-wees as you call him was going to kill a good Indian like Sau-en-quett."

"It's a matter of point of view, I guess. The Indians call Sau-en-quett bad, and Cush-a-wees good. He was defending Indian rights."

"Langdon, I'm beginning to wonder if you came along with these Indians to obstruct justice."

"All these Indians want is to be left alone."

"Then they'll have to learn to be farmers like everybody else, or get out of here and go west."

"Why?" Martin watched the squad of cavalrymen as they followed Chee-chee-qua after the Indians who had receded into the forest.

"This is farming country, Langdon. The east has to eat — wheat,

Langdon. You know that. This is where wheat can be grown. Look at yourself. You're a farmer, aren't you?"

"I'm a farmer — I guess you'd call me a pioneer," Martin admitted. "I came out here for cheap land, after being a schoolteacher back in York state. But others out here are merchants, and they're making the Michigan plow in a little factory in Grannisville."

"These Indians will have to go west unless they learn to live like white men."

"Had you ever thought of living in India, just as the Hindus do, Mr. Butler?"

"Of course not."

"Well that's what you expect these Indians to do — live like us, you say. But they're not like us. For a thousand years or more they've been living one way and we another."

"There's no room for savages this side of the Mississippi river," Butler snapped.

"You mean they're to be dispossessed of their lands?"

"Be a white man, Langdon. They'll be taken care of, but not here. They obstruct progress."

"And what of my wife?"

"How can she be affected, pray tell?"

"She's a half-breed."

"If she's your legal wife and wants to live like a civilized woman she'd be permitted to stay."

"And her father?"

"If he's an Indian he'll have to go."

"Perhaps she'd go with her father."

"Then you'd simply have to find yourself another wife. You're young. I'm sure you'd have no trouble."

Martin said nothing to this. He had no desire to have another wife. He and Owaysa were in love — had been from the day they met. He left Butler without saying good-bye and mounted his horse.

When he overtook the Indians encamped west of Allen's Prairie, he felt it incumbent to search out Chief Baw Beese.

"Chief Baw Beese," he said, "there's trouble ahead."

"I know."

Martin dismounted, and held the reins of his horse.

"I mean real trouble. The government is bent on sending you people west."

"But we no go."

"Then better forget about this law of the knife."

"No forget," said the chief. "Council voted . . . all old men and wise men decide on law. Sau-en-quett must die!"

"But that's murder now."

"It not murder when my daughter Wenona killed by Negnaska's brother. That what you say, 'execution'. She kill husband, husband's brother kill her."

"That was different. It was before Michigan was a state. Now it's murder."

"Not among Injuns."

"Just the same, unless you want trouble, you stop Kakatoma."

"Kakatoma gone now. Can't find."

The chief looked vaguely away, and Martin knew his request was futile. The chief would not listen to him.

"This Injun country," Chief Baw Beese said. "We do what want with Injuns. Paleface not care."

"This time it's different. A false move and they'll send you away."

"No!" The chief stood proudly erect. "Me, Baw Beese, no go!"

Martin hoped Pamasaw could prevail where he had failed, in his plea. "Where's Pamasaw?"

"Pamasaw, he lovesick. He leave for Moquago's village. Got girl there — want wife." The chief smiled knowingly.

"I wish I could see him. Which way did he go?"

"You know — Moquago's village. Girl is Moquago's daughter."

"I know." Martin gathered the reins preparatory to jumping in the saddle. "I must see him."

"No, please!" Chief Baw Beese restrained him by putting his hand on his arm. "Pamasaw in love. He think only love. He not help. Nobody help. You want soften law of tribe. No can change—nobody change. Sau-en-quett know law. He break."

"But they'll use it as an excuse that you're a troublesome people."

Chief Baw Beese shook his head.

"No turn back from vote of tribal council. That is law — good or bad. This time mebbe bad, but no turn back."

Martin was silent, and mounted his horse.

"You no stay here?" Chief Baw Beese inquired. "It late, no get back to village tonight."

"I'm not staying. I'm going home," said Martin.

So saying he wheeled his horse out of the Indian camp and continued east on the Chicago turnpike through Allen's prairie and Grannisville, then south on the Maumee trail through Hillsdale, to his own little cabin.

It was dark when his lathering horse pulled up to his cabin door, but Owaysa was waiting to greet him. For a moment he held her in his arms.

"How's everything been?" he asked.

"All right, Martin. I just got through milking the cow."

"The Indians have a law of the knife, Owaysa."

"I know that law. Who is to be executed?"

"Sau-en-quett! He deeded Mick-e-sawbe to the United States — against the wishes of the council."

"Then he will have to die!"

Owaysa accompanied him as he led the horse to the barn and unsaddled him. He rubbed him down good, before letting him drink even a little of the cold water at the spring.

By the light of the candle lantern he finished taking care of the horse, and bedded him down for the night, as Owaysa told him of the events of the day. She had done the chores, made some butter, and had hoed a little in the corn.

Then she inquired, "They sold nothing but Mick-e-sawbe, did they?"

"That's all — and Sau-en-quett sold that."

"Then it's still well with us and the people of the Baw Beese band!" she said.

They walked to the cabin, the rays of the lantern not needed as the moon rose over the hills to the east, and cast its mellow glow on the green growing things of the earth.

At the door they paused.

"It's good to have you home again, Martin. I missed you last night."

"And it's good to be home, Owaysa. But I wish you'd talk your Indian friends out of this law of the knife."

"Why?"

"Because, Owaysa, it means trouble for all of us. They'll surely use it as an excuse that all the Potowatomi must be moved west."

"Not yet, Martin. It's Indian country yet — so long as only Mick-e-sawbe is sold." He looked into the hazy distance in the moonlight, but said nothing, until she asked, "Isn't it?"

"Yes," he answered, holding her close to him. "It's still Indian country—right here. But the earth is good, and the Yankee pioneers want it. And some day it won't be Indian country any more."

4

The Course Of Love At Nottawa Seepe

Pamasaw struck off for Nottawa Seepe with the Moquago band, instead of going along with his father and the others towards Allen's Prairie and Grannisville. But the progress of the cortege was too slow for him, and urging his pony on the trail he had known so long, he soon found himself well ahead of the others. He wanted to reach the village before Wenojah should receive the bad news.

"I should be proud to have my daughter wed to the son of Baw Beese," Moquago had told Pamasaw. "But it is *her* heart you must win and not mine."

Pamasaw was sure that Wenojah loved him; but there was that ridiculous vow! Even as he rode it was obvious that there were more settlers along the trail every time he traversed it. Surely Wenojah must see the error of such a ridiculous declaration as she made to her father, within hearing of her suitor: "I shall never marry until the Long Knives have stopped invading our country. I, your daughter, Meadowlark, can keep my pledge to the manitou who has made me promise, even if I should die an old and withered maiden."

But today, as Pamasaw rode he fingered in his mind the 6 holes of his little wooden flute. He had planned the melody completely, and could hear the plaintive tones now as though he was actually playing the little instrument. It was a love song — and it was all he was taking today. There would be no other present — just this new melody.

When he reached the village of Nottawa Seepe, he found Wenojah making some moccasins as her mother was dressing a deerskin.

Wenojah, the Meadowlark, was dressed in ordinary deerskin with a short skirt, a jacket gathered around her lithe waist by a beaded belt, and a necklace of colored beads around her neck. Her hair was neatly plaited in two braids, and she pretended to be very busy working on the moccasins. Picking up a colored quill she placed it carefully across the toe of the moccasin, before anchoring it with bast.

Pamasaw hobbled his pony with the reins of his bridle — a pale-face sort of bridle that he had traded two beaver pelts for with Morgan, the storekeeper in Grannisville.

He did not approach closer to Wenojah, however. Instead he sat on the ground, pulled out his flute, and carefully placed his mouth over the tube at the upper end of the instrument. Not many members of the Huron-Potowatomi tribe could play the flute at all, and none could play better than Pamasaw. When he began his melody Wenojah's mother found it expedient to retire into the lodge, taking the deerskin with her. The tune was simple, containing only a few phrases, low, slow and soft, but to Pamasaw it expressed his feelings as he poured his heart out to his beloved, in this melody without words.

At first Wenojah looked down at her work, but finally she looked Pamasaw full in the face, her dark eyes expressing the admiration he had long wanted to see. Her two braids of hair which she wore in front seemed longer and blacker than they had ever seemed before, and she smiled at him. It was this smile he had longed to see from that far off day in Chicago when Wenojah had seemingly ceased to smile. That was five years ago.

"That's a pretty melody you've invented, Pamasaw," she said when he had finished.

"You think so? I am glad. It is for you alone."

Encouraged by her smile and compliment he tucked the flute away, arose and walking to her side, dropped on the grass beside her. Her nearness thrilled his heart, which beat altogether too fast for comfort. He longed to touch her, to encircle her in his arms.

"You bring news from Mick-e-sawbe?"

"I bring you only my melody, Wenojah!"

The Meadowlark sat silent a moment, concentrating her attention on the decorative quill she had just attached to the moccasin.

"But you've been to Mick-e-sawbe?"

Pamasaw looked at the soft green forest, and heard the gentle murmur of Nottawa creek. He wished to talk of love — his love, and not of Mick-e-sawbe — at least not yet.

"The melody, Wenojah, speaks as my heart speaks . . . ."

"Then your heart is very sad, for the melody is sad," she interrupted. "The news from Mick-e-sawbe is not good?"

"Your father will tell you of Mick-e-sawbe, and what must be done about it. But he knows of my love for you, and how I long to take you to my lodge at Ko-jess-sug-wa-seepe, in the dense forests where only the members of the band of Baw Beese can be seen."

"Only Huron-Potowatomi, Pamasaw? Are you sure?"

"There are only a few white families near there — nice people, named Champlin, and . . . ."

"Nice white people, Pamasaw? You have my answer."

"And it is yes, Wenojah? Your eyes are like two bright stars on a summer evening, and I know your heart beats for me."

"But it no longer beats with hope, Pamasaw."

"Why should it lose hope as it beats? Your love for me, and mine for you — the answer is easy. We need wait no longer."

"You know my vow — what my manitou said in my vision. I shall be miserable if I disobey the manitou. There'll be no happiness in our marriage unless every Long Knife is driven out of the land of our fathers."

"That can be done only by the manitou or all the spirits and ghosts of the forests." More and more Long Knives are coming.

"The great Tecumseh many winters ago could foresee that. That's why our fathers joined him to help the British drive the Long Knives back. Where is there another Tecumseh?"

Wenojah looked at Pamasaw as though hoping he would declare himself the embodiment of a new Tecumseh — a man who, like the great Shawnee, would lead his people. This time it would be to real victory over the white invaders.

"But your vow has no more basis in fact than the end of the rainbow, and its treasure."

"You are the man I could love, Pamasaw, if only you could see that the Long Knives are taking all from us."

"I can see they're taking away part of our forests, Wenojah. But we are powerless to do anything about it. We are as rabbits running before the wolves."

"Tecumseh did not run. He united many Indians, and if only a few more had come, and his orders had . . . ."

"Listen, Wenojah, Black Hawk tried that only the year before the treaty of Chicago, and he failed. There are too many Long Knives. We must learn to live with them — and be at peace with them."

"They don't want to live with us, either at peace or otherwise. Have you seen their women in their long skirts?"

Pamasaw nodded.

"And have you noticed how they swish them as though we were field mice whenever they meet an Indian?"

"I've never noticed that."

"You only pretend you haven't noticed it, Pamasaw."

"I don't pretend. I've never noticed their skirts swishing."

"Maybe you haven't noticed because you think they are pretty, with their pale faces. Have you noticed those with yellow hair—like corn tassels?"

"Yes, I've seen them, but they're not my idea of pretty women."

"How awful they look — sick, like drooping daisies after they're picked and allowed to wilt."

"I hadn't noticed them that much — Pamasaw has eyes only for you, Wenojah."

"Better you had eyes for what is going on around us, and see how the Long Knives treat us. They act as though we were strange beasts to be looked at and shunned, or laughed at."

"Not all Long Knives, Wenojah."

"Well, from what I've seen of them I know they don't want us to live in the same forests with them. What did they try to do at Mick-e-sawbe — take it away from our people?"

Pamasaw looked into the distance. The leaves on the nearest trees fluttered, and the branches moved like a sigh on the breeze. A sigh that would be echoed by all the people of Nottawa Seepe when they knew what had happened that day at Branch.

"You don't answer me, Pamasaw. Why not?"

"It is something your father should tell you."

"It is better that I know the truth. Since you tell me that you love me there should be no secrets between us."

Wenojah, the Meadowlark, looked very beautiful and pensive as she resumed her work on the moccasins. Pamasaw felt that the sighing of the wind in the trees was like the sighing of the manitous of the forest over the deed and treachery of Sau-en-quett. He was silent for some time. Finally he arose to his full height.

"Mick-e-sawbe was sold by Sau-en-quett to the Long Knives!"

"Sold, for how much?" Wenojah dropped the moccasin and looked straight ahead.

"For some whiskey, and that was destroyed."

"Whiskey? Was that all?"

"But he never got to drink it. The rest of us chopped up the barrels."

"Then we get nothing for Mick-e-sawbe?"

"Kakatoma will kill Sau-en-quett for signing the treaty."

"You must tell me about it."

Wenojah was excited by the news, and listened intently as Pamasaw unfolded the tale of the doings at Branch, and of the selling of Happy Waters. But as he told her of the stabbing of Cush-a-wees by Sau-en-quett's wife, she interrupted him.

"She's bad! Worse than even a woman of the Long Knives! She should be tried for murder before the council!"

"Perhaps," but when he told her of the agreement of the tribe to honor the treaty signed by Sau-en-quett she said: "It is a good thing that he should die. He's half white, most always drunk and consorting with Long Knives in their taverns. My father will reward Kakatoma."

"The Long Knives want to arrest him for attempted murder. He's hiding somewhere!"

"For murder? What about Sau-en-quett's wife killing Cush-a-wees?"

"They didn't care about that."

For a few moments they sat silently looking at the trees of the forest, and once again the leaves rustled in the breeze.

"Listen, Pamasaw. Do you hear the ghosts of Tecumseh's warriors speaking? They say the time has come when not a single paleface shall set foot at Happy Waters."

Pamasaw looked at her and shook his head.

"No, Wenojah, it's not the ghosts of Tecumseh's warriors that you hear. Your father and my father were both among those men, and they both know that the Long Knives are many — and what we hear are the footsteps of pioneers coming in numbers like blackbirds in a cornfield."

"You're defeated before you even go to battle. If you would win my heart you must be brave, Pamasaw."

"The days of the warrior are past. The Long Knives are here and we must live with them, or go to the land of the setting sun—the land of the Sioux, who hate us worse than do the Long Knives."

"I choose not to believe the son of Chief Baw Beese." Wenojah, the Meadowlark, arose and held her head proudly high. "He does not know that these forests are his — given to him by the great manitou forever. The forests are not for the palefaces. They cut them down, and saw the trees into boards—they make waste places where what they call wheat is planted. The Great Manitous do not like this, and the ghosts of all the Indians who have died to save their homes will have their revenge upon the palefaces for it. And yet you dare ask me, a chief's daughter, to live with people like that!"

Pamasaw arose now and spoke softly, pleadingly. "You will always have to live with the palefaces. They aren't all bad."

"Name me one good one! Just one!"

"Martin Langdon is one!"

"One among hundreds — thousands!"

"I can name others among the settlers."

"Settlers! They take our lands and pay nothing!"

"My father collects rent from some of them."

"How many?"

"Not many, Wenojah."

"There you have said it! That's the answer to your good Long Knives! For one good one there are a hundred bad ones. And the men! Do you know what they call me whenever I go into their villages! A squaw! Pamasaw, a squaw! That's what they call me, Pamasaw, a squaw! Me a single girl, called a squaw. And it's not even a word in our language!"

"When I am with you they will not call you a squaw. That's a Seneca word."

"It's a term that's insulting! They leer at me and say something like 'You're a right pert squaw. How about you and me going out in the woods together?'. I never heard them say anything like that to one of their white women with their pink cheeks. And these are the people you tell me I'm to live with? I will die first!"

She threw herself on the ground and glared at him.

"I had a sister named Wauneta who was to marry a paleface. He was killed by a bear in the forest when he was on his way to get a blackrobe to marry them. Well, Wauneta loved her French trader so dearly that she killed herself rather than live without him."

"I can't see how Wauneta could so far forget herself as to love a paleface. It's a wonder you don't find some girl with corn tassel hair — you're so fond of them — or would they laugh at you, Pamasaw, as their men laugh at me?"

Wenojah laughed half hysterically, as she arose from where she had thrown herself, and she faced him boldly. "And to think an Indian brave can speak to me of love, and then tell me I have to live with palefaces! I shall have no husband if there are Long Knives in our forests! I remember when we held our forests in peace and were let alone."

"Listen, Wenojah, I too can remember when there were no paleface villages here, although I was very young. I can remember when Moses Allen first set up his home at Allen's Prairie. But that was a long time ago. Now we have to change our ways. We don't have to be like the Long Knives, but we have to live with them, in the same forests."

"Soon there will be no forests! Just stumps and houses — and barns — big red barns, blotting out the beautiful trees. There'll only be plowed fields, only part of which will be growing corn."

"I know. All these things are coming every day. But we don't have to be afraid. The Great Manitou can take care of us. We can always have some of our forests."

"And live like conquered enemies? Like slaves? No, Pamasaw, it were better that we all join the ghosts of our ancestors than to have everything we own taken from us by our enemies — and they *are* our enemies, Pamasaw, be very sure of that."

"I prefer to wait and see to joining the spirits of my ancestors right now."

"Instead of waiting, rise up — all the Indians together can stop these Long Knives from coming into our domain."

"Wenojah, only your manitou can guide you. But I think you've listened too long to the tales of old women. I tell you, Tecumseh failed, and he is dead. His braves are either old or dead. There is no new Tecumseh, and there never will be. Pontiac failed before Tecumseh failed, and Blackhawk failed after him. So far as armies are concerned we cannot win, and I am not the man to try it, nor to stir up an uprising!"

Wenojah stooped to the ground, picked up her sewing, and started towards the wigwam. She turned when the mournful cortege of Moquago began straggling into the village, with the wailing proclamations: "Mick-e-sawbe is sold! Happy Waters is sold!"

5

The Hunter And The Hunted

There were two hunted men in the forests of southern Michigan that June night in 1838. One, a half-breed, the sub-chief Sau-en-quett, knew that unless his pursuer was hunted down and jailed, that sooner or later his enemy would be upon him.

The other man, a full-blooded Huron-Potowatomi, still possessed the long knife. His was the task of bringing tribal justice on the may who had disgracefully sold the beautiful reservation at Happy Waters. But he too was being hunted — by Sau-en-quett's wife, and a squad of cavalrymen. He must find his enemy before the soldiers found him.

Neither man could be sure where the other was. Kakatoma had first the problem of getting away from the pursuing army men, and must flee to terrain unfamiliar to him, or at least not in his customary haunts near Nottawa Seepe.

Sau-en-quett had merely to hide in some spot not likely to be thought of by Kakatoma. But even then, his life could not be wholly safe. For he now knew that despite his boasting at the council fire there was one who would willingly wield the knife that he had ridiculed. Furthermore, Sau-en-quett was half drunk with whiskey given him by Warren at the government agent's request. Sau-en-quett had never been a hunted man before. He had always been the hunter—the boaster. Mostly men had listened to his superior knowledge because he was half French.

Sau-en-quett could read and write. He had gained this small knowledge from a French priest but in no other way had he been able to absorb any sort of religion or fine manners from the French side of his ancestry, unless it was his indubitable cleverness and shrewdness. It was stupid of his fellow chiefs, he believed, to try to obstruct the inroads of the Long Knives. Better do as he said. "Get the best price possible for the land." Only a fool could believe they wouldn't take it any way. The Long Knives always took everything they wanted. Better take their whiskey and have what fun one could than to fight them.

That Tecumseh fellow, years before, what had he achieved? A chance to die fighting the Long Knives somewhere in Canada. That's all it had gotten him. And only a few years ago what had Black Hawk achieved, only to be ignominiously captured, and placed on exhibit like an animal in a zoo.

Being an Indian brave was all well and good, but it was better to boast about it in the taverns of the Long Knives than to go on the warpath. In fact, so far as Sau-en-quett could determine most of the old Indian trails and paths in his part of the country had become well worn and rutted roads traveled by the pioneers.

But now matters were different. For some time he had been known as a sub-chief among the Huron-Potowatomi, and as a big chief among the Long Knives. His largesse in gracefully ceding them Mick-e-sawbe, his own village, should accord him some honor among the palefaces. But now there were his own people to face, with that law of the knife they had invoked. This, he had not foreseen. He had only thought of favors from the Long Knives.

And they could still show him favors, if only they could catch this Kakatoma before Kakatoma could catch *him.* Then, as he skulked off in the woods, south of Branch, he began to think of the fact that even if he escaped Kakatoma, he might still fall victim to the law of the knife — some day, somewhere. There was one hope only — that Kakatoma's arrest would so frighten them that the tribal council would annul its decision to put the law into effect.

* * * * *

In the meantime Kakatoma was in hiding not far from Branch. He watched the cavalrymen led by Chee-chee-qua ride off in the direction of his home near Nottawa Seepe.

Kakatoma smiled, and sheathed the long knife in his belt. If anybody thought he would be stupid enough to go anywhere near his own home at a time when he was being hunted they were not worth worrying about. He came out from his hiding place behind a fallen tree, and skirted the environs of the tavern. All seemed serene there but he wondered if Sau-en-quett were still inside. He must carry out the will of the tribe — the law. He was all Indian — a grandson of one of Tecumseh's most trusted warriors. Ah, to be like Tecumseh, and win not only the admiration of his own tribe, but to be able to unite all the Indians against these invading Long Knives. Some failed in this attempt only because they acted too fast. If Tecumseh could have had time enough to unite all the Indians east of the Mississippi then the Long Knives might have been held out of these forests. He remembered Black Hawk, and had felt disappointed that his own tribe had not beat the war drums. But this was just as well, for Black Hawk was far from ready. Tecumseh had the British for an ally. Black Hawk had nobody. To win, one must have all the Indians — even the hated Sioux across the Mississippi. Getting them to help would not be easy unless he could perhaps marry into their tribe. But the Sioux might slit his throat if he ventured into their country. All this was nebulous dreaming. His first duty belonged to the tribal council of the assembled bands of Moquago and Baw Beese. There could be nothing further in achieving the dreams of his people until he could get rid of Sau-en-quett. There was the daughter of Moquago — Wenojah. She would admire him if he could prove himself brave enough. There was a chance that she might marry him if he could succeed in this dream of promoting a general Indian uprising.

But he must be very cautious about this. Pamasaw, son of Chief Baw Beese, who could read and write in English, was a favored suitor. Pamasaw, who had no dreams of Indian greatness — believed in getting along with the Long Knives as best he could. But Kakatoma knew that Wenojah, the Meadowlark, had refused to marry so long as the Long Knives were in this country.

Driving them out would be almost impossible. There were now so many. But with properly laid plans and the right kind of military aid, possibly from Canada, it could be done. Kakatoma watched the tavern closely for any trace of Sau-en-quett. But there was no sign in evidence. He dare not go inside alone, to investigate. Butler would be in there, as well as Warren, and it was best that they believe him to be far away right now.

Kakatoma could not believe that his quarry had left the tavern. He must be very drunk by now, and would be an easy prey to the knife he carried. But yet he hesitated. Twice he considered going inside, and then thought better of it. Finally, creeping cautiously toward the tavern, he peered in the small window. There was no sign of Sau-en-quett. There was Josiah Butler sitting in a chair, talking solemnly with Warren. Kakatoma meant to be out of sight before being seen just as Butler looked up to behold him peering through the window.

"Look!" Butler pointed at the window. "There's that red devil now!"

Kakatoma scurried away, but on hearing the tavern door open he fell on his hands and knees. When the shot from the musket was heard, the ball whistled over his head. He lay motionless only a second.

"Get him?" asked Butler.

"Guess so! He's lying still," Warren's voice answered.

Kakatoma had fallen so he could see the men at the tavern door. Only Warren held a gun, and he had fired it and missed. Triumphantly Kakatoma arose from the ground, and, giving a taunting yell, dashed off into the forest.

He couldn't be positive, but he felt reasonably certain that Sau-en-quett was no longer in the tavern. Covering his tracks would pose a problem, but he would try. In any event he must put space between himself and the tavern. He dashed off in the woods in the general direction of Masonville, should Chee-chee-qua and the soldiers return, or even Warren take up the chase. By going northerly in this direction and then circling south of the tavern he felt reasonably safe from any immediate discovery.

He began to search the ground for telltale signs of other Indians, chiefly Sau-en-quett, who was wearing paleface boots with his otherwise complete Indian regalia. Sure enough there were footprints in the scarce grasses under the trees. They were either Sau-en-quett's or some white man's track. Since there were no other tracks around, and these led away from the direction of the tavern, Kakatoma concluded they must have been made by Sau-en-quett.

He could hear horsemen in the distance and concluded that Chee-chee-qua and the soldiers had returned from a fruitless search for him. It was right then for him to have gone north from the tavern, and then circle south. Chee-chee-qua probably could track him — in fact would do so in a matter of time. He must overtake Sau-en-quett before this happened. It was easy to fool the Long Knives unless they had an Indian guide along to enable them to read the signs made by moccasined feet in the forests, as all Indians could—even the quas. He could only hope that the footsteps he was following were those of Sau-en-quett.

* * * * *

SAU-EN-QUETT finally had decided where to go. He had shuffled along some time before he remembered a tumble-down bark hut on an island in the big lake to the south. It wasn't really an island, and although entirely surrounded by swamp and water there was also a way onto it. He hoped that his footprints were not too obvious. Anyhow, he was wearing paleface boots. Possibly Kakatoma and the other Indians would never know those footprints were his.

It was growing dark when he reached the edge of the lake. He was weary, and the effects of the firewater in the tavern were wearing off. He wished he had more. But there was no firewater in this area. Sau-en-quett hoped there were neither white men nor red men to see him going to the island. Before he reached the water's edge he found at last a little-used trail. There he had the presence of mind to start walking backwards. In that way his footprints would be pointing in the direction from which he came. He was still walking backwards when he stepped off into the ooze of the swamp. Then he turned, and made his way to the decaying bark house some Indian had long ago abandoned and left to rot. He was tired, and once inside he fell upon the ground, exhausted. Before he had spent so much time in the taverns he was tougher – could have stood this walk much better.

He felt reasonably safe and secure, but he dared not sleep. He wished he had a pistol. But then, he was never very good at shooting a pistol. Probably just as well, he concluded, as he pulled out of his belt the green-handled knife that Chee-chee-qua had used in killing Cush-a-wees back at Branch.

The knife now in his hand, he was ready for any emergency but try as he could to stay awake, he was drowsy. The whippoorwills were calling, but there was no sound of approaching human feet. He lay with an ear on the ground to warn him of any such possibility.

He vaguely wondered if he was to spend the rest of his life in this furtive manner, always fearful of falling asleep. If only Chee-

chee-qua were with him she could stand guard while he slept. But Chee-chee-qua was busy hunting down his enemy, Kakatoma. His enemy? Was Kakatoma his only enemy, or the whole tribe of the Huron-Potowatomi? Sau-en-quett could not be sure — could never be sure. He would be much safer, perhaps in the taverns of the Long Knives. They would have to protect him. But he had been afraid to stay at the tavern in Branch.

Probably he was safe here. At least he hoped he was, and finally, he could stay awake no longer and fell asleep.

* * * * *

KAKATOMA made good time following the shuffling footsteps he had found in the forest. Appearing on the trail the footsteps were still easily discernible. He even saw exactly where the footsteps were reversed and could tell by the imprints they were made by a man walking backwards. Now he knew he was following Sau-en-quett, who wanted to confuse or deceive a pursuer.

Sounds behind Kakatoma indicated that there were horses in the distance. He placed his ear to the ground. That would be the cavalrymen. They had found his trail — Chee-chee-qua had tracked him.

When he reached the edge of the swamp he unhesitatingly entered it where the other footprints had looked as though a man had gone out. That would be the island, so he went cautiously forward. The sound of the horses was coming closer, as he reached solid ground. The whippoorwills had just seemingly settled down for the night. By the light of the rising moon he saw the old bark house, and fell on his knees stealthily. He crept towards it, breathing slowly and exhaling carefully to silence even the faintest noise. Once he struck a twig which broke and set off a series of sounds in the forest from wild creatures. But these soon subsided. By now the horsemen had reached the edge of the swamp. Here Kakatoma realized the horses could not travel. They would be mired down.

He reached the door of the bark house. Inside was a man lying on his belly. The light was clear enough so that it was obvious he was in the regalia of a chief. His breathing was heavy.

Silently Kakatoma pulled the long knife from his belt. He continued to creep towards the slumbering Sau-en-quett. Once the steady breathing stopped, and he made a convulsive movement.

Kakatoma stood erect, raised the knife high, and fell with all his force, thrusting the long steel blade into Sau-en-quett's back. It came through his chest.

Sau-en-quett raised up and fell down dead. He had made only a gasp.

Kakatoma heard the soldiers wading into the swamp, guided by soft whispers from Chee-chee-qua. He leaped from the ruins of the bark house, and out to the water side of the island. There he slid into the lake and began to swim.

He could hear the soldiers in the distance, he could hear the wail of Chee-chee-qua, and once he heard his name called.

But Kakatoma was far out in the lake by then, completely invisible from the island.

He had performed the execution. He would be a hero in the tribe forever, whenever the council fires of the Huron-Potowatomi were built and old men told their tales.

6

The Mystery Of The Manitou

When Kakatoma arrived at the cabin of Martin and Owaysa they did not know that Sau-en-quett was dead; but Martin was dubious about giving sanctuary to the Indian.

He had glided into the cabin without knocking and sat down without invitation. He was naked to the waist and wore silver bracelets on his arms like Pamasaw. His hair was short in accordance with the custom. His buckskin leggings were torn and stained, but otherwise he did not appear bedraggled.

Martin looked up from the book he was reading by candlelight and Owaysa paused in her sewing as she was patching some blue jeans.

"Baw Beese say me stay here. Be your hired man," said Kakatoma.

"I can't afford a hired man," Martin answered.

"The chief asked me today if he might hide out here," Owaysa said. "He can't stay among his own people with the officers pursuing him."

"Me get no pay — but work real good." Kakatoma smiled hopefully.

"You'll have to wear blue jeans and look like a hired man if I let you stay. And you'll have to sleep in the barn."

Kakatoma frowned as though he wanted to object to this proposition and was beginning to remonstrate.

"Me never wear pale face clothes," he grumbled.

"It's the only way you can hide, Kakatoma."

"Work, but no wear paleface clothes."

"Then you can't stay here." Martin arose and began filling his pipe from the tobacco jar on the mantel of the fireplace.

Kakatoma looked sullen. "Where go?" he asked.

"Sau-en-quett's little qua will see that you go to jail," Martin tamped the tobacco in his pipe, and reached for a small stick to light in the fire.

"Here, Kakatoma!" Owaysa tossed the blue jeans she had been patching to the young Indian. "You wear these and a shirt, or we'll tell Baw Beese you can't hide here."

Kakatoma looked at the paleface cloth with distaste and swallowed as though he had actually been fed bitter medicine. But he took the garment, and rising, glided out of the room and into the night.

* * * * *

The next morning when Martin went to drive the cow into the barn, he found Kakatoma wearing the patched blue jeans.

"Shirt," said the Indian. "Must have shirt!"

Martin procured one later that morning, and together they began hoeing the diminutive corn. But as time went on and the June days became longer, Martin could see that Kakatoma had little interest in agriculture, working more or less ineffectually and never with any enthusiasm. Owaysa too seemed somewhat changed. She took to absenting herself from the cabin, giving no explanation of her whereabouts.

Sometimes both Owaysa and Kakatoma would be absent together, then again only one of them would be missing from the farm for several hours. Martin wondered if the pair were meeting clandestinely. But he was unaware that they had so much in common until one day while the three of them were eating dinner he said, "The corn'll be knee high by the Fourth of July."

Kakatoma and Owaysa looked at him, but instead of making a comment on his remark began conversing in Potowatomi — something they frequently did.

It was at such times that Martin felt a strange gulf seemingly broadening between his own world and that of his wife's. This was his house. This was his farm. Owaysa was his legal wife; but it was increasingly obvious that a racial tie existed between Kakatoma and Owaysa.

They shared a common language, only a few words of which were comprehendible to Martin. And as time went on he seemed to be almost a guest in his own home — at his own table.

Finally, Martin inquired irrately: "Can't you find anything to talk about with me, Owaysa?"

She only looked at him, and did not answer. Instead she arose from her chair and began to clear the table. Kakatoma glided out the door, and Martin was glad to be alone with his wife.

"What does it all mean, Owaysa—why are you so strange lately?" Martin arose and stood close to her.

"Strange, Martin? In what way?"

"You seem to ignore me, lately. All your attention turns to Kakatoma."

"That is not true. It's only that — well there are Injun affairs that you know nothing about — need know nothing about."

"What kind of talk is that?" Martin asked petulantly. "I'm your husband. No need to keep secrets from me."

"You wouldn't understand!"

"Can't you trust me any more?"

"Of course!"

"Then why is it that you can't talk to me, and you run off by yourself so much? It's too early to gather berries in the forests. None are ripe."

"Sometimes Martin, I have to talk with my soul — my Injun soul — my manitou!"

"Manitou!" He released her in astonishment. "Don't tell me you have one of those imaginative things too—like Pamasaw! Pamasaw's manitou told him to marry the daughter of a great chief at a distance. Pamasaw has decided he must marry Wenojah. She won't have him because there are palefaces in Michigan, or until they're all driven out. It's my guess Pamasaw's in for a long wait."

"But wait he must—until Wenojah's manitou shows her a different way — unless Pamasaw gives her up."

Martin tried hard not to show his violent reaction over such a strange belief, for Owaysa took such matters for granted — like the sunrise, and the seasons. She continued stacking the cooking utensils into a pan.

"Then explain it to me," he said. But Owaysa refused further comment. After she had finished piling up the dishes she took them over to a little shelf where a pail of water stood, and began to wash them in silence. He was tempted to shake her into telling him the truth. But he suddenly remembered that he had been understanding about the edicts of Pamasaw's manitou, whereas in the case of his wife's same strange belief he was impatient; and since the silence was evidently not to be broken by Owaysa he arose and strode out the cabin door.

A man of action rather than one who long brooded over his wrongs, imagined or real, Martin found it difficult to sit at meals and hear Kakatoma and Owaysa conversing in a language he did not understand; and more difficult to refrain from chiding her for excluding him from their conversation.

Concluding that there must be a connection between Owaysa's manitou and Kakatoma, he was becoming suspicious, and decided the Indian must go.

How he could bring this about, however, posed other problems. If he drove Kakatoma away, and he fell into the clutches of the law both Chief Moquago and Baw Beese would be angry; and furthermore, should Kakatoma tell where he had been, he would be accused of harboring a criminal. If these things transpired he would have enemies where now he had friends, and in the precarious environment of the pioneer, Martin realized he could not afford enemies both red and white.

But the presence of Kakatoma and Owaysa's superstitious veneration of her manitou was increasingly onerous. Both must be eliminated if possible. However, there seemed no way of getting rid of the Indian, and no way presented itself to bring Owaysa back from her Indian ways. For the next couple of days he worked with his problems, hoeing corn viciously, but seeking to be as pleasant as possible.

Then, at dinner, just as Kakatoma spoke something in Potowatomi to Owaysa, Martin interrupted bluntly.

"There's a celebration tomorrow in Grannisville."

"A celebration?" Owaysa turned to him curiously.

"It's the Fourth of July you know."

"Well, what of it?" She shrugged, and speaking in Potowatomi, passed the beans to Kakatoma. Martin was irritated.

"It's the celebration of the Independence of the United States from England."

"Oh, the United States celebrates that, does it?"

"Owaysa, you know it does! There have been celebrations before!" Martin dropped his fork on his plate with a loud jangle.

"Yes, Martin, I know. But when will the Indians celebrate their independence from the United States?"

Martin said nothing but resumed eating in silence while Kakatoma smiled ingratiatingly at Owaysa, asked for more cornbread, and spoke in Potowatomi. But Owaysa was silent and sullen, avoiding Martin's steady gaze.

When the meal was ended and Kakatoma had gone out the cabin door, Martin arose and crossed to Owaysa who was hastily gathering up the few dishes.

"What's coming over us, Owaysa" What's coming between us—is it Kakatoma?"

"You should know better. Sometimes you talk like a little boy."

Martin looked at her a moment, then walked to the door. In the doorway he turned and said in a commanding tone: "Tomorrow I'm going to Grannisville to that celebration. You are going with me!"

Kakatoma was already hoeing corn near the house when Martin went outside and picked up his hoe. Today he would watch his wife to see where she went.

When Owaysa left the cabin, she was dressed in her buckskin garb, and looking neither to the right nor the left she walked to the edge of the forest, and was lost to view.

"Wife go talk to manitou," Kakatoma said by way of conversation.

"Where is he?" Martin asked quickly. "What's he like?"

"Who knows?" Kakatoma shrugged. "Mebbe bear—mebbe turtle—mebbe . . . ."

"A Man!" Martin expostulated. He looked sharply at the Indian.

"Choo-ween!" said Kakatoma. "She not with man!"

Kakatoma's superior disdain was irksome. He, an Indian, spoke as though he considered Martin utterly ignorant.

"Then who the hell is she going to see?"

"Injun must go to woods — alone. Then manitou come — tell her what's what. Injun must be alone — alone in woods — sometimes."

"You hoe corn, Kakatoma. I'm going to see this manitou that's advising my wife!"

He leaned his hoe against a stump and started off in the direction Owaysa had taken. Kakatoma laughed softly after him, and Martin heard him say, "You won't see manitou."

When his crude boots had bitten into the last of the soft dirt in the cornfield, and he had reached the point in the woods where Owaysa had vanished, he became more cautious, and moved as silently as an Indian — so quiet was his approach that not even a squirrel chattered at him. The path was not new, and Martin followed it only a short distance through the trees when he came upon a glade. He paused behind the thick trunk of a maple tree and peered cautiously at his wife.

Owaysa was sitting silently on a large stone, unaware of his presence so near to her. She was so still and silent that she hardly seemed to breathe. Then her eyes would occasionally scan the blue sky above, and then as silent as before seemed only to be listening. But there was only the sighing of the wind in the trees, punctuated with the song of a robin, a cardinal, or the distant cawing of a crow.

He watched her for some time in silence, then crept away half ashamed as though he had been watching some sort of sacred ritual that he had been seeking to destroy. It had been foolish of him to be jealous and suspicious. He retraced his steps to the cornfield, picked up the hoe quietly and began work.

"You saw?" Kakatoma inquired.

"I saw."

After working in silence for a time, Kakatoma said: "Injun must be alone — must talk to manitou — then, mebbe manitou talk to Injun."

"But why does Owaysa do this now? She never ran off like this before you came here."

"She not need to talk to manitou until now."

"You mean she's wishing she'd married an Indian?"

"No!"

"Then what do you mean?" Martin whacked viciously at the grasses growing in the knee-high corn.

"She talk — the trees talk — talk Injun language."

Martin was exasperated.

"She said nothing!"

"No words — voice inside! It come to Injun in woods."

"Now I've heard the final nonsense. My wife hears voices! First I heard there was a panther in my spring — a white panther. It was pulled up out of the spring by some medicine men one day. They shot it, and got its blood, then it ran away to the lake that's shaped like a boot. It lives there — nobody ever saw it, but it lives there."

"Mebbe it come out!"

"Yes," Martin said with resignation. "I expected to hear that next. What then?"

"It come out to hurt people — maybe take Owaysa back in lake with him. But mebbe thunderbirds come, scare panther back. Thunderbird Injuns' grandfather."

This was too much for Martin. Could Owaysa too believe this superstition? Tomorrow he would go to Grannisville where there were palefaces, people like himself — civilized people who took no stock in manitous, white panthers or thunderbirds. Owaysa was going with him. He must get her into a white man's world somehow — a world she seemed to be forgetting, now that Kakatoma had come.

"Tomorrow, Kakatoma, I'm going to Grannisville to the celebration. You're not to come, do you hear?"

"Me hear!" Kakatoma resumed hoeing the corn.

"I'm taking Owaysa with me," Martin said, and leaned on his hoe, awaiting a reply from the Indian.

"She not go!"

Martin smiled. "Who's the boss among the Indians?"

Kakatoma hesitated, stopped hoeing the corn, and looked Martin in the eye. "The brave, he boss!"

"I'm the only brave, Kakatoma, that Owaysa has. Understand that!"

Martin hoed weeds imaginary and real from the corn, as though he were rooting out every Indian superstition that had ever existed in this land that was now becoming a farm, but that had until his coming, known only the moccasined feet of red men.

* * * * *

The next morning at breakfast Owaysa was silent as had become her custom of late. Martin laid his fork on his plate and stated simply, "Owaysa, we're going to the celebration."

"You go, Martin. There's nothing to celebrate." Owaysa continued eating.

"No, we're both going."

"I don't belong there, Martin. I belong in the forest."

"There's to be a big ball game – Indian ball. The Indians are helping in the celebration."

"Indians have nothing to celebrate. No, I won't go!"

Martin arose from the table and looked at her. "So you plan on going into the woods and communing with your manitou – you're going to pretend you're really a full-blooded Indian?"

"Martin, I . . . ." She looked up at him as he towered above her. Her eyes flashed defiance.

"Then we'll play Indian all the way. Owaysa! I'm your brave and you're my qua! You'll do as I say and go to Grannisville!"

Owaysa said nothing as she stood up and began clearing the table. She silently took the dishes outside the cabin and started to wash them in a pan on a slab at the end of one log. Martin followed her out, and his voice was commanding – harsh.

"You heard me, Owaysa! Get ready! Wear the blue dress my sister sent you from Buffalo."

Owaysa bowed her head to her task, but Martin knew there would be no further refusal. "I'll saddle the gelding," he said. "Do you want a saddle?"

"No!" she snapped. "Don't forget I'm an Injun! I'll ride like one!"

Tossing her head defiantly she carried some of the dishes back into the cabin, and Martin went to the barn. He saddled the chestnut gelding, and then fastened a blanket on the bald-faced mare.

He had a feeling of triumph as he stepped into the cabin to don his best clothes. He was, however, immediately taken aback when he saw Owaysa preparing to wear her Indian finery. He frowned as she slid the soft white deerskin shirt over her head and down around her hips.

"I told you to wear the blue dress," he said, getting out of his blue jeans, and picking up his pantaloons.

She slipped on the white deerskin jacket. Her hair was in two braids in the tradition of Indian women.

"Don't you like me dressed like this? The first time you ever kissed me I was wearing deerskin."

Martin looked at his wife. He had to admit that she was about as beautiful in white deerskin – more so actually, than she would have looked in blue. Pulling on his pantaloons, he struggled to his feet, and drew her into his arms and held her so close that she could hardly breathe.

"What's been wrong with you, Owaysa — why are you acting so strange?"

"It's this latest land grab," she said.

"Land grab?" He freed her and finished dressing.

"Yes! The United States is acting as though the Indians don't exist. They're dividing up land as though nobody lived on it at all."

"And what has that to do with us — you and me?" He pulled on his coat.

"There'll soon be nothing left for my father's people. They'll be crowded off the land. That's what it has to do with us."

"I'll take care of Osseo when that time comes, Owaysa. You know I will."

"What of the others — Chief Baw Beese, Ash-te-wette, Pamasaw, or even Kakatoma?"

Martin said he didn't know, bent down and strapped his pantaloons to the instep of his boots.

"My manitou tells me it will all come to a bad end, Martin. There can be much bloodshed. Whose will it be?"

Martin stood erect and, putting his hands on her shoulder, spoke sharply. "I wish you'd stop talking about your manitou. You act as though the thing really existed. You know it's just superstition."

"Is it?"

"Yes! It's against the church — it's against God to talk that way, after a Christian marriage!"

"Why?" Owaysa's dark eyes looked squarely into his blue ones.

"I can't tell you why. I only know you're my wife — I love you and I want you to keep on loving me — instead of paying attention to superstitious nonsense. Come, let's get started."

Once outside they mounted their horses and started up the Maumee trail to the village of Hillsdale. As they reached Howder's tavern, Owaysa said: "They're trying to move the county seat over here aren't they?"

"They'll never do it. Grannisville is on the old Sauk trail, and look at this location here."

"When I was a little girl there was no Hillsdale, nor Grannisville, nor even Allen's Prairie. I remember only Tecumseh."

"In twelve short years — from forest wilderness to settlements," thought Martin now fully awake to the situation.

"Invaders! That's all the Long Knives are. Once it was all beautiful forests with only a few fields and orchards. Now there are villages with sawmills devouring trees. Some of the settlers are even burning their part of the forest. It's all very wicked, Martin, and it's not as the creator intended."

"Nothing can stop it, Owaysa. It's progress — a sort of onward march of thousands — seeking freedom from lack — freedom from domination — and — well, just freedom!"

7

In Which Martin Learns That Kakatoma Is A Murderer

At Howder's tavern they were joined by several settlers who came from the woods and clearings, all headed for the big celebration at Grannisville.

Some were clad in rude buckskins, but the women were dressed in cloth skirts, and the group now numbered about a dozen people, all of whom Owaysa had known. However, there was a newcomer from the tavern, whom Martin had never seen before.

He was riding a prancing dapple gray horse, and he wore a battered, old army uniform, much patched, and he was hatless. Guiding his spirited animal to Martin and Owaysa, it was obvious he had been drinking heavily.

"Howdy, Stranger," he greeted. "Headin' fer the celebration I'll bet."

"That's right," said Martin. "You a settler in these parts?"

"Yup! Name's Maxon – Ed Maxon. Took up land 'tother day. Trouble is there's a damned Injun village on it." As Owaysa looked sharply at him, he began to hedge. "No offense meant, miss. This your girl, Stranger?"

Martin answered, "This, Mr. Maxon, is my wife. My name's Martin Langdon. Have a place south of here."

"Your wife, eh? Well, well, well!" He looked at Owaysa appraisingly. "Glad to meet yuh, Mis' Langdon."

Owaysa did not acknowledge the greeting. Instead she drew closer to Martin and motioned with her head to get away from Maxon.

"I don't like him," she whispered. "He's going to make trouble."

"You think so?" he asked, eyeing Maxon, who appeared not to notice their conversation.

"He's bought that land purposely where Ko-jess-sug-wa-seepe is built."

Martin nodded.

"Got to get those Injuns off my farm afore I kin do anything on my place," said Maxon. "Goin' to find out in Grannisville today what I kin do about it."

"Why didn't you take up land somewhere else?"

"Because the Injuns have cleared about 20 acres fer me without knowin' it." He laughed. "I'm an Injun fighter — been one all my life, but my 'pologies to you, Mrs. Langdon. I don't fight with squaws . . . no sirree!"

Martin said nothing, but realized that Owaysa had spoken the truth.

"Never kin trust an Injun!" Maxon continued. "They're a thievin' murderin' lot. But then I cal'late you already know that, livin' out here. Ben here long?"

"About six years," Martin said. "Yes, it was six years ago this month I first came here, and met my wife."

"You don't say! Been married to Mrs. Langdon here all that time?"

"Most of it!"

"Well, well, well, who'd have thunk it!"

Martin was finding the conversation somewhat annoying, and turned to Owaysa. "I'll race you to the creek," he said.

Owaysa said nothing, but signalled the bald-faced mare into a gallop, with Martin in pursuit, leaving the others behind in the dust of the rutted road.

When they had reached the little creek over which the pioneers had built a wooden bridge, Owaysa, who was in the lead, reined in her horse and turned to Martin.

"Did you hear what he said about Ko-jess-sug-wa-seepe?"

"Of course."

"Do you see now why the Indians have nothing to celebrate today?" She paused but Martin did not answer her. "He says he's an Indian fighter," she continued. "And did you notice that old uniform he was wearing? How old is it?"

"Couldn't say, Owaysa. Probably from the war."*

As they continued on their way to Grannisville more settlers and their wives and children poured out of the forests along the road, and joined what was now a cavalcade.

* NOTE: This would be the War of 1812, referred to at this time in history, only as "the war."

It was on the edge of the village that Owaysa and Martin were overtaken by the thundering hoofs of the dapple gray horse, and Maxon, his head thrust forward, holding an imaginary saber was yelling: "Charge! Go right through the damned redskins! Whoopee!"

In a cloud of dust the drunken old soldier disappeared into the village itself, and both the mounts of Martin and Owaysa, becoming restive, attempted to take pursuit, for no horse seemingly wants another horse to get anywhere ahead of him.

Their animals were still unruly from the restraint imposed on them when they arrived in the village, which was indeed in festive array.

Not even the holiday was halting the flow of emigrant traffic along the Chicago Turnpike, but many a yoke of oxen and horse-drawn covered wagon was decked out with special holiday decoration, some carrying flags. The Great Sauk Inn was almost concealed by the temporary speaker's platform in front of it.

All appeared to be in good-natured tumult and confusion, with gamblers playing the old three-shell game, and old Goon-pa-shee — she of more than the hundred winters — seated in a tent announcing in a quavering voice to passersby: "Goon-pa-shee know all — tell all!"

Throughout the settlement the teams of emigrants, lumber wagons of the settlers, even some buggies, but mostly saddle horses were tied to saplings, and the crowd milled about, greeting old friends, gathering to see a Punch and Judy show, watching the three-shell game of the gamblers, or listening to the fortunes as told by Goon-pa-shee.

Dismounting their horses and tying them, Martin and Owaysa started down the street. Owaysa clung to Martin, suddenly timid, and wide-eyed at this large number of strangers.

Together they made their way over to the old Indian woman who was a self-professed fortune teller. Goon-pa-shee, looking straight ahead as though reading invisible writing in the air was saying to a young couple before her: "You be unhappy here! You marry, but go back to land of fathers, that way!" She pointed eastward.

The girl shrugged, and the gay young man in a swallow-tail coat said: "I can't go back east. Tildy wouldn't have me if I did, would you, Tildy?"

"I will go where you go, Henry," Tildy, a buxom lass of twenty dimpled.

The couple walked away, their spirits undampened, as Goon-pa-shee placed a silver coin in a leather bag, and mumbled to herself.

"How do you dare tell fortunes when it's been prohibited by the tribal council?" Owaysa demanded.

Old Goon-pa-shee smiled knowingly. "Chief Baw Beese and council not care what tell paleface. Besides make-um *shuniah."*

Then the face of the old woman changed to a look of apprehension and fear, as another couple was approaching. It was Pamasaw and an Indian girl in finer deerskins than those worn by Owaysa.

"Martin, this is Wenojah!" Pamasaw said. "And this, Wenojah, is Owaysa, Martin's wife."

Wenojah said only "Posho!" She did not smile.

"She can't speak English," Pamasaw explained.

Goon-pa-shee uttered a few baleful phrases in the Huron-Potowatomi tongue, pointing an accusing finger at Pamasaw, then blowing on her shrivelled fingers, as though blowing away dust.

Pamasaw did not smile at this performance, and Wenojah looked displeased.

"She said that Wenojah and I will bring sadness to my father, causing the entire tribe to be blown away as the west wind blows the dust before him," Pamasaw explained.

Both Wenojah and Owaysa seemed uneasy at this statement by Goon-pa-shee, but Pamasaw, less apprehensive, drew Martin aside and inquired: "Kakatoma didn't come did he?"

"No!"

"Good. Wenojah says officers from Branch are looking for him here. Did he tell you how he stabbed Sau-en-quett in the back?"

"What?" Martin was astonished. "Did he kill him?"

"Of course. The law of the knife, you know."

"When?"

"Why, the night after the treaty was signed at Branch — out on an island in the big lake, it was."

"Then all this time we've been harboring a murderer?"

"No, an executioner."

"He's a murderer, Pamasaw. This isn't Indian country any more!" Martin turned to Owaysa. "Did you know this, Owaysa?"

She nodded that she did.

"So that explains it!" he expostulated, so loud that passersby stopped and looked at him curiously. Noticing this, Martin spoke under his breath. "That's why you've been talking together. You ought to have told me, Owaysa."

"You wouldn't have let him stay," Owaysa said. "He's only done his duty by the tribe."

"And put us in jeopardy!" said Martin.

The four of them began to move away from Goon-pa-shee. Martin was angry about the deception. "I thought he was only wanted because he had *tried* to kill Sau-en-quett. Now I'm guilty of harboring a criminal."

"Please Martin, people will hear you," Owaysa cautioned.

"And suppose they do. Suppose I turn him in, as I've a mind to. What then?"

They were drawing near the speaker's stand in front of the inn, and a disconsolate Indian with a patch where his nose should be was brought out on the platform by Sheriff VanHoevenbergh.

"Leathernose has been a bad Indian," Pamasaw said to Martin. "He was caught with another man's wife. So his nose was cut off."

"Indian law?" asked Martin.

"Indian law."

"Hear ye! Hear ye!" the sheriff bellowed. "We're about to hold court on the Fourth of July, in the year of Our Lord, 1838, with the Honorable Justice of the Peace, John Taylor, presiding."

The justice of the peace mounted the platform majestically.

Placing his tall hat on the table, he cleared his throat several times and sat down, as the crowd became silent and attentive.

"I'm ready for the complainant," Justice Taylor said.

"Ed Bushnell!" Sheriff VanHoevenbergh bellowed.

"Here!" a pioneer's voice answered, and a stalwart man, tanned from exposure to the elements, but dressed in the customary pantaloons, tall hat and tails, made his way to the platform.

"Raise your right hand," the sheriff commanded Bushnell, who obeyed. "Do you solemnly swear before these people here assembled and the Honorable Justice John Taylor, that the testimony you're about to give shall be the truth, the whole truth and nothing but the truth, so help you God?"

"I swear it."

Justice Taylor read the complaint before him, after taking out some iron-rimmed spectacles and polishing them with his coat tail. He looked up and said: "Mr. Bushnell, will you please tell us in plain and simple language just what this Indian has been up to?"

"Your Honor, he's been digging up the wheat in my wheatfield."

"No!" Leathernose shouted angrily. "Me plant corn in my own cornfield!"

"Silence!" Justice Taylor scowled at the Indian. "The prisoner will speak when he's spoken to."

Leathernose was about to retort, when Sheriff VanHoevenbergh said: "Shut up, you. You're in a court of law."

"Law!" a voice Martin recognized as that of James Kinman spoke from the crowd. "You can't hold a trial on the Fourth of July."

"Who says so?" Justice Taylor shouted.

"I do!" Kinman came to the platform. "This is a legal holiday!"

"Anything's legal if I say it is," Justice Taylor said. "I'm justice of the peace here and these Indians will have to learn a lesson."

"I'm his counsel."

"His counsel? You mean he's retained you?"

"I'm the counsel of any Indian who needs me — have been ever since Chief Baw Beese helped our family through a sick spell." Kinman climbed up the steps and onto the speaker's platform.

"I don't see what you expect to gain by this, Mr. Kinman. This fellow doesn't have any money, and the complaint plainly says he's planted wheat in Ed Bushnell's cornfield. That's right isn't it, Ed?"

"Of course it's right."

"Then the sentence will be . . . ."

"I object, your Honor!" Kinman said. "The man's not been proved guilty."

"Quiet! Mr. Kinman, I'll have you cited for contempt of court if your interruptions continue."

"Do you know the procedure, Justice Taylor?"

Taylor was becoming exasperated. "Kinman, here's a simple case of an Indian violating the law and planting corn in a settler's wheatfield."

"May I ask him a question?"

"Only one."

"My man, did you or did you not plant your corn in Bushnell's wheatfield?"

"Always plant corn there! *My* cornfield!"

"Then your Honor, the Indian pleads not guilty."

"Not guilty?" Bushnell roared. "He's a damned liar!"

"Here, here, Mr. Bushnell! You can't use such language before the court." Justice Taylor rapped the table sharply with his fist, and then looked at his bruised knuckles.

"Well, it's my field! I bought the property at the land office in Monroe."

"My cornfield!" Leathernose stolidly insisted.

"The court finds the defendant, known as Leathernose, guilty!"

Leathernose scowled, and Kinman objected, but Justice Taylor continued. "You're not to plant corn in Mr. Bushnell's wheatfield."

"Then where plant um corn? All rest fields got big trees."

"Then don't plant any!"

"Injun get hungry — no corn."

"Then go to work!" shouted Justice Taylor rising. "Court's adjourned."

"Just a moment," Kinman said. "I have entered a plea of not guilty for my client."

"And I've found him guilty, Mr. Kinman. I'm the law here. Be thankful I haven't fined him court costs, and you too."

Justice Taylor strode angrily into the Great Sauk Inn, and Sheriff VonHoevenbergh said to Leathernose, "Be off with you."

"But what Injun eat?" Leathernose looked about pathetically.

"Do like the rest of the people. Find yourself something to do and earn money. Make baskets, but don't raise corn!"

The sheriff left the platform, leaving the disconsolate Leathernose and his erstwhile attorney standing together.

8

A Game Of Indian Ball

It was at the precise moment when Leathernose was sullenly leaving the platform, that Martin saw Chee-chee-qua, accompanied by a tall, broad-shouldered white man, making her way through the crowd and pointing.

"He there! He there!"

"Come, Owaysa, I can't face her. That's Sau-en-quett's wife." He attempted to lose himself, but the little Indian woman had reached him.

"You!" she said addressing Martin. "You see him?"

"Who?" Martin parried.

"Kakatoma!"

Martin knew she was going to ask that, but pretended surprise. "Kakatoma?" he asked.

"He's not here!" Owaysa said emphatically.

"This man, he deputy sheriff . . . you know big law . . . in Branch! He help find Kakatoma!" Chee-chee-qua said.

"Know him, Stranger?" the white man inquired.

"Well, I — I can't say that any white man knows an Indian." Martin avoided a direct answer. It was all different, now that he knew Kakatoma was wanted for murder and not just because he had threatened to kill a man. He could not and would not condone murder, but neither did he wish to be involved in the consequences of harboring a criminal. Governor Mason had intervened for him in the Territorial days when he had been wrongfully accused. But this time he could not rely on the same governor's understanding in this matter.

The deputy sheriff, however, was not to be so easily put off. "I mean," he said. "Do you know him when you see him?"

"I daresay I would."

"Is he here today?"

"I haven't seen him here," Martin could answer this question directly and unequivocally.

"This man's a bad Injun," said the deputy. "He murdered a man in cold blood out on the island in Coldwater Lake."

"Sorry to hear it," and Martin was sincere in his statement.

"If you see him, remember I'm lookin' for him," said the deputy, moving away, and Martin had a feeling of relief at being saved further questioning. He did not like to lie, directly, but neither did he wish to become involved with the law.

Although Pamasaw and Wenojah had been standing close by, Pamasaw had managed to hide behind other people in the crowd, and had not been detected by Chee-chee-qua.

The sullen Leathernose brushed against Martin, and Wenojah said something in the Potowatomi tongue, but Pamasaw shook his head.

"What did she say?" Martin asked.

"She said for Leathernose to throw his knife at Bushnell," said Owaysa. "She says there are enough Injuns here to drive the Long Knives back where they came from."

"Well, I vum!" It was the voice of Filena Van Duzer. "Did you hear that, Ellen?"

The blonde young woman, looking disdainfully at Martin and Owaysa, answered, "What else can you expect of Injuns, Ma?"

"I hope, Ellen, you don't plan on calling out the militia," Owaysa said.

"Could be a good idea. I did it once, you know."

Martin recalled his past troubles, when Ellen had accused him of stirring up the Indians. But Owaysa was a match for Ellen.

"Got too much hair in your head today, Ellen?"

Ellen looked at Owaysa in dismay. It was evident she had not forgotten the episode in which a handful of her hair had been pulled out by the roots."*

"Come Ma, let's get out of here. We belong with white folks."

Ellen tugged at her mother's sleeve, looking at Martin in annoyance, drew her skirt disdainfully around her, and she and her mother

*NOTE: This episode is recounted in the author's *Curse of the White Panther.*

left with as much hauteur as the big crowd permitted.

"I can't stand her!" Owaysa was furious. "I wish . . . ."

"Don't bother about it now." Martin patted her hand on his arm. "I don't like her too well myself. And always remember, you got me. She didn't."

For the first time in the past few weeks Owaysa smiled at him.

"Where's that there Judge?" a man's voice called out, and Maxon lurched towards the platform.

"I wanna see the judge!" he bellowed.

Sheriff VanHoevenbergh came forward, and took Maxon roughly by the arm.

"Le' go of me. You aint the judge!"

"No, but I'm the sheriff. What do you want of Judge Taylor?"

"Wanna tell him how danged right he was puttin' that Injun out o' that wheatfield. I got problems too — only I got a thousand Injuns in my wheatfield."

"You mean Squawfield?" Pamasaw came forward belligerently.

"Guess so. It's my field, and I want . . . ."

Pamasaw was enraged. Wenojah began hurling Indian invectives and Maxon began retreating into the crowd.

It was then that George Grannis came out on the platform and announced: "Ladies and Gentlemen! We were to have as our speaker, the Rev. Darius Barker, the new rector of Grace Church, but I've been unable to find hide nor hair of him."

"Well, I'm here!" a voice shouted from the crowd, and the Rev. Mr. Barker, a tall young man, wearing a black swallow-tail coat and broad-brimmed black hat came to the foot of the platform and began climbing onto it.

When he reached the table, he looked out on the crowd and smiled.

"As I understand," he began, "I'm the first man who has had a chance to speak from a platform in the open air in this county. Even the great Daniel Webster, they tell me, when he spoke at Moscow, was compelled to use for his platform only a stump. So I should feel deeply honored."

There was a spattering of applause, and as he paused Martin saw the grinning face of Kakatoma, at the edge of the crowd.

"Come!" he said to Owaysa, under his breath. "He's here!"

"Who?"

"Kakatoma! I don't know whether to turn him in or not!"

"What do you mean?" Owaysa inquired in a whisper so loud that nearby people looked at her, and even the Rev. Mr. Barker paused and gazed in their direction. But Kakatoma had vanished from sight, as Martin attempted to drag his wife along to the edge of the crowd.

"But I want to hear the speaker," she parried.

"No you don't," Martin said in an undertone. "You don't want to talk to me alone."

What the speaker had to say at the celebration neither Martin nor Owaysa could ever know, for he guided her deftly out of earshot.

"I want to know," Martin said to her when they were in a secluded spot under a tree and the speaker's voice was droning in the distance, "just why you've deceived me. You knew all along that Kakatoma had murdered Sau-en-quett!"

"But he didn't murder him, Martin. He merely executed him according to our law."

"Owaysa, you're my wife, and when you say 'our law', you must remember from my standpoint it's Indian law, and Indian law is NOT the law of the land!"

"Please, Martin. I told you the Indians have nothing to celebrate today!"

"But you didn't tell me that we were shielding a criminal! I thought we were only protecting him until that difficulty at Branch blew over."

"It never will."

"And do you realize now that I know the truth it puts us in a dreadful light? They might even accuse us of planning the crime. I can't understand you, Owaysa."

"Nor I you."

"And furthermore, he's come here today. Chee-chee-qua is here too, and if he's captured, which sooner or later he will be, he'll tell where he's been hiding . . . ."

"Kakatoma won't betray his friends."

"That remains to be seen. And now I know what you've been talking about in that Indian language of yours; discussing a plan, I suppose, and all the time I thought — well, no matter what I thought. I still can't understand how you'd expose me to such a risk."

"It's no risk. You're well thought of here, and . . . ."

As their argument continued they heard the crowd applaud, as the speaker left the platform. George Grannis then appeared and waved the crowd to silence.

His voice in the distance announced: "It's time now for that game you've been waiting for – the ball game between the Moquago and the Baw Beese bands!"

There were lusty cheers and even some shouting. The goal posts with nets were spaced along the turnpike in front of the dwellings and stores for a distance of about a hundred yards. The Indians came forward carrying their bats holding little nets at the end. Their faces were painted as though they were going into warfare and there were fully thirty players on a side.

George Grannis himself was the referee, who placed the little ball on the ground in the center of the field. He gave a loud whistle, stepped back, and both teams scrambled forward in their attempt to get the little ball scooped up into the nets of their own players.

Suddenly Martin clutched Owaysa by the arm. "There's Kakatoma!" he muttered. "The fool! What's he playing for?"

The ball went out of bounds into Morgan's store, but instead of stopping the game, Grannis let it proceed, and all the players went in after it, creating great havoc among the piled blankets. And then when it came outside, it next found its way into a settler's cabin, across the street. It still had not approached either goal and George Grannis was breathless trying to stop the play, when a scream from the crowd rent the air.

It was Chee-chee-qua, crying: "There he is! There he is!" She began running through the crowd and into the excited players, followed by the pistol-waving deputy sheriff of Branch county. But Kakatoma was quick to notice the commotion. He dodged among the Indians, darted through the spectators, and off to the north of the village.

"Stop him!" shouted the deputy, who now fired his pistol at the leaping Kakatoma. The shot went wild and with the pistol fired the deputy had no time to reload. Nobody tried to stop the fleeing Indian.

The crowd had never seen the deputy before, nor Chee-chee-qua. They assumed it was some Indian problem and cheered in unison when one of the pioneers yelled: "On with the ball game!"

And as though nothing had happend to interfere, the Indians of both bands pitched violently into the game. There were fouls. Players were knocked flat and unconscious. They hooked their sticks together in an effort to obtain the ball, and violated almost every rule, but in the end the Baw Beese band won the game by five goals.

It was not until the excitement of the game was over that the deputy, after a futile pursuit of Kakatoma, mounted the platform and shouted to the crowd: "I want a posse!"

The loud voice brought momentary silence, and he continued. "That Indian is wanted for murder! Do you hear me, murder?"

Chee-chee-qua wailed loudly: "He keel my husband! He keel Sau-en-quett!"

There was hardly a stir of interest. Sau-en-quett was not a name with which they were familiar.

"You, there, VanHoevenbergh!" the deputy shouted. "Get me a posse!"

"Who'd he kill, some Injun?" VanHoevenbergh asked.

"Sure he killed an Indian! A good Indian!"

"Then let the Injuns catch him!" countered the sheriff. "Never figured it was my business to meddle into Injun killings!"

The deputy sheriff from Branch county and Sau-en-quett's widow were unsuccessful in raising a posse on that Fourth of July. It was the only celebration of the year, and the pioneers were going to make the most of it. Posses over Indian affairs might be well and good at other times. But not today.

And at dusk they congregated in the Great Sauk Inn and danced until the red dawn was streaking across the sky.

9

Some Neighbors Come By Ox Cart

The sun was rising in the east when Martin and Owaysa were wending their way homeward on the Maumee trail, and although they had danced all night with the rest of the revelers, Martin's spirits were high. Owaysa was acting almost like her old self.

Kakatoma's unexpected appearance in full Indian attire in the ball team gave him a feeling of relief from an unjust responsibility. The Indian was gone, and with him went his worries.

"I do wish, Owaysa, that you'd worn the blue dress instead of your Indian outfit," he finally said.

"Does it matter now? Nobody refused to dance with me."

"That has nothing to do with what I'd like to say. It puzzles me that you never emphasize your mother's line of descent."

"You knew what I was when you married me, Martin. I was brought up according to Indian custom."

"I know – but there was the Seneca wife Tabor brought with him. She wasn't wearing *her* Indian garb."

"Huh, *THAT* woman! Tall, scrawny, and almost black! Did she look beautiful in that dress?"

Martin laughed. "No! I was only thinking how you'd have outshone every other settler's wife in your blue dress."

"But I'm not a settler, Martin. I've always lived here. She comes from a reservation in New York state."

Martin made no reply. Why was Owaysa so stubborn? She was—why she was as stubborn as an Indian! He laughed to himself at the old, well-known adage usually applied to a mule.

After the manner of horses nearing home, the bald-faced mare and the sorrel gelding became so restive that further conversation was impossible.

"I'll race you home!" said Owaysa.

Martin, letting her get a head start held his nervous gelding in check for a few seconds before accepting the challenge, and together they sped over the rutted road that had once been only an Indian trail.

The air was invigorating. The sky was cloudless but the morning mists were rising from the forests along the way. Life was good. His lovely Owaysa — his cabin — seemed the center of the earth just now. He'd been resentful, that's true, against Owaysa because she had not told him about Kakatoma's crime, but that no longer mattered; thank heaven he had disappeared.

By this time they had reached their destination and had dismounted from their horses when Kakatoma — in his blue jeans and shirt — appeared in the farmyard. He stepped forward and took the reins of each horse.

"Me take horses! Big day! Big night, huh?" He was grinning as though nothing had happened.

Martin was completely non-plussed, devoid of any ability to decide what to do, or how to proceed. All he could do was to blurt out, "You! — you can't stay here any more!"

"Me stay! A-owh!" and Kakatoma led the horses to the barn.

Martin, turning to Owaysa, said, "But he can't — he's got to get out of here!"

"Please, Martin! You forget! Chief Baw Beese has promised him protection."

"Then let Chief Baw Beese protect him!"

"But remember — the land — this land! Chief Baw Beese gave it to you. It wouldn't be right to go against his wishes."

Martin turned and followed her into the cabin. He was about to retort that the land was not actually the chief's to give, but checked himself. He sat down, and leaned back in his chair, staring straight ahead. The land office was selling the broad acres of forest and swamp of southern Michigan. It no longer belonged to the Indians, or if it did, the United States no longer recognized the Indian title.

"Owaysa," he finally said. "We can't shield Kakatoma. The wife of Sau-en-quett will surely look for him here. She recognized me. You saw that."

"But how can she know that . . . ?"

"I don't know. But she'll be here — I know it."

"But he can hide! And everybody knows his name is just Joe, and they will not . . . ."

He arose from his chair, and taking her by the shoulders looked straight at her."

"Owaysa! He can't stay. I'll not have it! Suppose that fellow, Maxon should recognize him!"

"He won't! He was too drunk!"

"Maybe, and maybe not!"

"Let me go, and I'll get us some breakfast. Anyhow, we have to change our clothes," said Owaysa, who evaded his grasp and immediately began removing her deerskin skirt and jacket.

Martin mechanically pulled off his pantaloons, and carefully hung up his one good suit. They ought to be tired, but the day was new. There was much work to be done.

They said nothing more as Owaysa put fresh wood on the fire and filled the kettle preparatory to boiling some water. It was customary for Martin to read a chapter from the Bible each morning before breakfast, usually picking out a chapter at random. Sometimes this method rewarded him with very little meaning or inspiration and today was one of those days and although his mind wandered, he forced himself to read to the end. If there was any message there, it consisted chiefly in the fact that there had been many generations of people accounted for in the Old Testament. Owaysa never asked questions during this ritual but when breakfast was ready and they sat down to eat, she asked, "Did you find any particular message or information?"

"Yes, in a way. There have been multitudes of people on this earth before us; there'll be multitudes more after us, but I'd like to stay out of trouble during our lifetime if I can."

"And Kakatoma spells trouble. Is that it?"

"We'd all breathe easier if Kakatoma gave himself up."

"Martin!" Owaysa looked up from her plate in disbelief.

"What else can he do? They'll catch him sooner or later."

"And he'll be killed when they do. Chief Baw Beese will know what to do. Anyhow, Kakatoma won't leave until the chief gives his consent."

"He went to the celebration yesterday and Chief Baw Beese certainly did not advise that."

"Promise me, Martin, that you won't send him away until you've talked with the chief."

Martin deliberated only a moment, and then acquiesced. He could chance harboring the Indian another day.

So intent were they on their own affairs that morning they had forgotten to call Kakatoma to breakfast, but soon he came in, glided to the table, and looked appealingly at Owaysa.

Martin studied the wooden dishes from which they were eating as though they had been graced with infinitely complicated designs. They were Indian made. He must send east for some decent china. He must cut some logs and have some timber sawed to frame a house. He must make some money from his wheat this year, to do these things. Yes, he could tolerate Kakatoma for one more day — just one. Then he must go.

Looking up he said, "We'll hoe corn again today — Joe!"

Kakatoma said nothing.

"And don't you ever forget that your name is Joe when anybody comes here — no matter who it is, even if it happens to be Chee-chee-qua."

"Me know!"

The corn was more than knee high, and the crop looked good. The little field of wheat was ready for the cradle. Kakatoma could be useful right now. He cost nothing but his keep, but in the eyes of the law he was a criminal, although the Indians regarded him only as an executioner.

It was shortly before noon when down the rutted road from Hillsdale, came a slowly plodding yoke of oxen drawing a cart. There was a canopy over the cart, and Martin could distinguish a woman in a sunbonnet riding with a baby in her arms. Beside the cart a man was walking, occasionally using the terms "Gee" or "Haw."

When Martin saw the equipage pulling into his yard he went down to meet the strangers.

The man was of medium height, broad-shouldered, with a floppy hat over his uncombed light brown hair, and eyes that were friendly and blue. Although the woman's hair was largely concealed by the sunbonnet, what one could see of it revealed dark curling wisps around the ears. She seemed a plain woman, but pleasant.

As Martin approached them the man extended his hand first. "Howdy! My name's Sam Pratt. This here's my wife Joanna, and the wee might in her arms is Ralph!"

Martin acknowledged the greeting, then after introducing himself, said: "It's about dinner time, and I suppose you are hungry. Will you join my wife and me?"

"Thank you, Mr. Langdon. That's very kind." Mrs. Pratt smiled and was starting to get down from the ox cart when Kakatoma appeared. She clutched the infant closely to her, and hurriedly resumed her place in the cart.

"This is my hired man — Joe," Martin smiled. "Joe, this is Mr. and Mrs. Pratt."

The Indian nodded stiffly, and started for the wash basin and water bucket at the flattened log.

"Owaysa!" Martin called. "We have company!"

Coming to the doorway, Owaysa surveyed the newcomers.

"You're welcome," she said, and added, "if you like peas and new potatoes and Indian-baked beans."

"Indian baked beans, what are they?" Pratt wanted to know.

"Fixed with jerked bear meat, and seasoned with sassafras," Owaysa answered. "Martin learned to like them when he stayed at our lodge in the village."

"What village?" inquired Mrs. Pratt suspiciously.

"Meshawa-od-dawn," said Owaysa, who then vanished into the cabin.

Mrs. Pratt looked at her husband and whispered, shaking her head. Then Pratt spoke up: "Mr. Langdon, we're powerful hungry, and I figure we'd like a bit of rest, but my wife — er — well, she's kind of afraid of your hired man and your squaw."

"Just a minute, Pratt. She's my wife, not a squaw. We were married in a church at Tecumseh, if that's bothering you."

"Well, now no offense was intended. She's a mighty purty woman."

"Did you call her, Owaysa?" Mrs. Pratt inquired.

"That's her Indian name. Her Christian name's Delia."

"I like that better," said Mrs. Pratt.

Then followed the business of watering the oxen at the spring, tethering them so they might eat some of the lush grass, then the formality of washing hands and drying them on the towel outside the cabin and being joined by Kakatoma and then proceding inside the cabin. Martin realized it was the first white family to eat in his cabin during the three years it had been built. Owaysa made no apologies for the wooden dishes, but instead explained they were made by the Indians, with obvious pride.

"It appears to me," Sam Pratt observed, "that Injuns aren't so bad as we've been thinking."

"Some are good. Some are bad, just like other people."

"There was that Indian fella they was chasing around Grannisville yesterday," Pratt continued. "I guess he's a bad one."

Martin and Owaysa exchanged nervous glances, while Kakatoma concentrated on the beans. He was eating none of the peas and new potatoes which would have been foreign to his taste.

"Yes sir," Pratt narrated. "They've finally got the sheriff of Hillsdale county and a posse out now, scouring the woods. It took a powerful bit of explaining I guess. Because they say he only stabbed another Injun over in Branch county somewhere."

"Where did you people come from, Mr. Pratt?" Martin asked quickly, anxious to channel this explosive narration of so recent an event into a different vein.

"Call me Sam — we're from Painesville, Ohio."

"I was in Ohio once — Toledo, Ohio. But it was Michigan then. I was in the militia; and I've always thought we could have won that war if President Jackson hadn't switched governors on us, about time of our first battle."

"I was in the militia, too, only I was in the Ohio troops. We certainly had some janty uniforms, and did a lot of drilling. Bet we'd have won if there'd been a show-down. Only Michigan was using Injuns, and that scared us a wee bit."

"Were you in the surveying party under General Zachary Taylor — the outfit that ran thirty miles at the sound of a volley of musketry and rifles?" Martin inquired.

"Nope! Never got to Perryburg until the day it was over and Toledo was part of Ohio."

"Have some more beans, Mrs. Pratt," Owaysa urged, passing the dish to her.

"No thank you." She smiled. "They're all right I guess, but I can't seem to get used to the flavor."

"I couldn't either when Owaysa first fed them to me. But I had to eat what she cooked or go hungry. You see I had a broken leg when she met me and I couldn't get away," Martin explained.

Mrs. Pratt laughed pleasantly and remarked: "That's one way of getting a husband."

"If I recollect rightly, though, right at the time she tried pretty hard not to get me. In fact she threatened to shoot me when I arrived — because I was a white man. But she did get my interest."

"Would the baby like some milk?" Owaysa obviously wished to change the subject.

"He's quiet now. May I see if he'll sleep on the bed?" Owaysa led the way to the bed and Sam turned to Martin.

"Where's a good place to homestead?" he asked.

"You haven't been to the land office at Monroe?" Martin looked at Sam, although watching Owaysa as she assisted Mrs. Pratt, tenderly tucking the baby in the big bed not far from the table.

"I figured I'd find the place I want first," Sam was saying. "Then I can go to the land office later. They told me in Grannisville that just about everything out this way was wide open for settlers."

"They say the land sharks are snapping up some of it between here and Hillsdale," commented Martin.

"There are a lot of ways of dealing with land sharks — I hear."

"Such as . . . ?"

"Well," Pratt deliberated, looking around the table, then smiled, "of course there are the Injuns!"

Kakatoma suddenly stopped eating. He glowered at Sam Pratt, Sam's baby, and his wife. Then, saying nothing, he pushed back from the table, arose, and walked out of the cabin.

"Then too there are the wild animals — bears and panthers and the like. There are massasaugas — and, as I said — Indians."

"By all means the Indians!" Owaysa said. "We've always been the excuse for anything that goes wrong!"

"Now, now, Mrs. Langdon, I didn't mean that. I just mean . . . ."

"You've said more than enough, Sam," Mrs. Pratt stated.

"What you're saying, Sam," Martin hastened to add, "is that anything can happen out in the woods — but it doesn't generally occur nowadays. Land sharks have a legal right to operate."

"Chief Baw Beese and the tribal council own the land here," Owaysa said. "There's been no signed treaty."

"Then what do you mean, Langdon, about the land office in Monroe, and land sharks?"

"The land office is selling it any way, with or without a treaty."

"We'll cross that bridge when we come to it, as the old saying is. Know of a good eighty acres?"

"Almost anywhere south or west of here, I guess. But remember, I've warned you."

"How close?"

Martin saw Owaysa signaling him and knew she did not want these people too close by.

"Oh, say a mile west of here. But besides the land sharks you'll have to deal with Chief Baw Beese."

"Is he tough?"

"That depends on you. Treat him right, and you'll have no trouble."

"You say a mile west? But there's no road."

"Chop one through. That's how the other settlers are doing."

Sam Pratt smiled, and pushing his chair back from the table, stood up.

"Well, can't say that I'll enjoy it. But thanks for the help, Neighbor. Come on Joanna. Get Ralph bundled up, and we'll go west—but only for about a mile."

10

The New Neighbors Get A House

It was not until the day of the house-raising at Sam Pratt's that Kakatoma appeared again. He came with Pamasaw and other Indians Chief Baw Beese had sent to help erect the pioneer cabin.

Martin felt uneasy about Kakatoma the moment he saw him. Why had he suddenly put in an appearance after absenting himself from the neighborhood from the day that Pratt and his family had arrived?

Other homesteaders had come, none of them with deeds to their land. Martin had warned them individually that the homesteads were being snapped up by speculators, but still they continued pouring into the area, shrugging off the possibility that a land shark might claim title to their holdings.

Chief Baw Beese ingratiated himself by accepting each new family as though they had entered his domain at his behest. But the shrewd chief always bargained for a portion of the crops. Since many arrived too late to grow food for themselves they found themselves actually in debt to the Indians for provisions for the coming winter. Few pioneers had money enough to purchase supplies at the stores in either Grannisville or the little hamlet of Hillsdale.

So when Sam Pratt had come to see Martin to inform him he had sufficient timber cut for a log cabin, and asked his assistance, Martin agreed. He also sent word to his friend Pamasaw to have the chief send Indians to help.

"With these Indians helping," said Sam, "we can get it built in a hurry."

"What are you working with?" Martin asked.

"Mostly black ash, with the bark peeled off. Can't afford fancy stuff at Lockwood's sawmill."

So on the day in question — a bright, sunshiny day in early August, there were not only Indians aplenty, but some of the other pioneers as well. It was now a great event when a cabin was erected. No longer need a man struggle with the long logs alone, or with only a few friends.

Pamasaw was helping to put a log in place with one of the other Indians when there suddenly appeared Chief Moquago and his daughter Wenojah, and Pamasaw dropped the end of the log he was holding. But Wenojah either ignored him or did not see him, for both she and her father dismounted from their horses and went directly to Kakatoma.

Martin was making wooden pegs to hold the edifice together,and Kakatoma, coming over to him, said, "Wenojah and Chief Moquago say that sheriff come. Tell Chief Baw Beese I go back to land of Chippewa, or mebbe Ottowa. But go far."

Moquago had brought a spare horse and Kakatoma, mounting it, rode away with the chief and his daughter. The matter might have ended there, so far as Martin was concerned had not Pamasaw come over to him and said, "Wenojah is in love with Kakatoma."

"What makes you think so?"

"Because she told me one time Kakatoma has done something to help the Indians, and I'd done nothing."

"Maybe she's right. But you don't have sheriff's posses looking for you. Perhaps your knowledge of the English language will do more than Kakatoma's knife."

But Martin had barely finished talking when the sheriff and his men came into the stump-filled yard.

"Martin, I want to talk to you a minute," said the sheriff.

Martin stopped his work, after giving orders how to use the pegs, and stepped beside the sheriff's horse.

"Well, here I am," he said.

"Martin, you've been recognized."

"What do you mean?"

"That little widow of Sau-en-quett's! She saw you the day her husband was killed in Branch."

"Well?"

"I've heard that you've been hiring an Injun this summer."

"Any law against me having a hired man?"

"Not unless his name's Kakatoma."

"We called the man I hired Joe," Martin looked the sheriff squarely in the eye.

"A lot of Injuns are called Joe. I hope you know, Martin, the law's different now that we're a state."

"Of course," Martin agreed. "I know that. It's what we want isn't it? Civilization in the wilderness and all that?"

"Do we — or maybe I should ask, do you?"

"I've always thought so. I came out here to get a homestead and I've got one. That's what the rest of them who come want. It's what Sam Pratt wants."

"That's right, Martin. But I wouldn't be harboring a fellow that's wanted for murder if I were you."

"I understand."

"Which one of these Injuns is he?"

"If you mean Joe, he's gone."

"Where'd he go?"

"Said something about going to see some Chippewa. "You'd know him I suppose?"

"Can't rightly say," Sheriff VanHoevenbergh said. "Never knew too much about Injuns. To me, Martin, an Injun's an Injun, just like a fox is a fox. I suppose a fox's mother knows one pup from another, but I don't. And that's the way I feel about Injuns — Chief Baw Beese excepted. I can tell him all right. He's so big and fat."

"I've heard the Chippewa live up north of Jacksonburg," Martin said. "If you're curious about Joe you might . . . ."

"Oh, no! Unless we could get him before he gets north of our county line it wouldn't be worth my trouble. So long as he isn't here I'll take your word for the fact that he's gone into the north country. I'll admit I expected to find him here. Folks will talk, you know, Martin — even some of the Injuns. But if he's gone — well, I guess he's gone."

Martin heaved a sign of relief when the sheriff and his posse left the grounds and then turned to see how the work on the cabin was progressing. It was obvious that when it came night Sam Pratt and his family could leave their beds in the ox cart and sleep under their own roof.

* * * * *

When Kakatoma did not put in an appearance that night Martin and Owaysa believed he was gone for good.

"The sheriff knows who Joe is," Martin said as he sat down to breakfast the next morning.

"Are you sure?"

"I'd have to be pretty stupid not to know what he was talking about. I hope I never see that Indian again."

Further talk on the subject was forestalled by the entrance of Chief Baw Beese and Pamasaw, and Martin could see that they were both perturbed.

"Martin," Pamasaw announced breathlessly. "Our land's been sold."

"What land?"

"The land where Ko-jess-sug-wa-seepe stands!"

"You mean that fellow Maxon?"

"Yes. He said he'd bought it in Grannisville on the Fourth of July. Well, he showed us the deed. It's signed by Martin VanBuren." Pamasaw looked distraught.

"He come last night," Chief Baw Beese said. "He bring paper, and Pamasaw read um!"

The chief sank onto the bed in despair, and Owaysa offered Pamasaw a chair. "No, Owaysa. I'll sit on the floor — real Injun style."

When Owaysa asked some questions in the Potowatomi tongue, Chief Baw Beese became vindictive. As his anger mounted the words *"Kamochekit"* and *"me shup-shee"* were spoken loudly. The chief, forgetting himself, spit on the floor vehemently.

Martin forsook his breakfast, arose and spoke sharply to the chief.

"If you expect me to help you in this, you'll have to speak English."

"Owaysa says perhaps you can talk with Maxon," Pamasaw ventured.

"Perhaps better let young men burn cabin — drive away — mebbe kill him!"

"Now Baw Beese you know that'll serve no good purpose."

"But he say he burn our village — plow up place for wheat!"

"Like Bushnell did with Leathernose north of Grannisville," said Pamasaw.

Owaysa turned pleading eyes at Martin. "Can't you do something?"

"Then if he not listen—mebbe bear break in—kill Maxon!"

"Chief Baw Beese, I'm surprised that you, who are old and wise would think of such a thing. Bears wouldn't do that!"

"He has no right whatever to that land!" Pamasaw arose and strode to the fireplace. "Maybe if you talked to him he'd listen to you. You're a settler."

"Of course I've never seen him when he was sober," said Martin. "He didn't seem exactly amenable to suggestion on the Fourth, when I saw him at Grannisville."

"He did talk real mean," Owaysa began clearing the table of the breakfast things. "Didn't you see him shouting that he wanted his land cleared of Indians — like Bushnell?"

"He different when he have no firewater. Carry big pistol all time — and big knife. Afraid of big bear, or white panther, mebbe!" Chief Baw Beese smiled.

"Well, I'll go and see him," Martin acquiesced.

Owaysa immediately took his pistol from the mantle and began to load it.

"What are you doing?"

"It's better you take it — loaded!"

"Threats won't do. This requires a smooth tongue."

"If he's armed, Martin, you'd better be too. The village is deep in the woods — you know the law of the woods — or have you forgotten?"

Martin smiled and, taking the pistol, tucked it in the belt of his blue jeans.

"I'll be back as soon as I can," he said, and accompanied Pamasaw and the chief.

At Ko-jess-sug-wa-seepe, they were greeted by the customary barking of the wolf-like Indian dogs, joining in excitement of the moment, with their human masters; and as always, Martin was welcomed as the staunchest of friends.

Chief Baw Beese, pointing out a trail to the south of the village, said: "Maxon live down there. Best you go alone."

Riding to the south Martin soon came to the customary opening in the forest, some stumps and a log cabin. A woman was turning the wheel of a grindstone, while Maxon, in rough country attire, was sharpening a scythe.

Without pausing in his work, Maxon said: "Thought you was

one of them pesky Injuns. Well, what can I do for ye?"

Maxon leaned the scythe against the cabin.

Martin dismounted, and offered his hand. "Martin Langdon," he smiled. "You remember — I met you on the way to Grannisville, on the Fourth of July."

"Oh, yes!" It was plain that Maxon's memory of the occasion was somewhat foggy. "Well, happy to meet ye again, Langdon." He took Martin's hand and shook it heartily. Then he added, "This here's my wife Azuba." Maxon pronounced the name Azuby.

"I see you're busy. Haying?"

"Yeah, got some marsh grass to cut. Can't get any other. Fact is, my farm's overrun with wild Injuns."

"Oh?"

"Yeah! Got a purty field with fifteen acres, more or less, and what you think? Them pesky redskins is campin' on it."

"And where's that?"

"You come by it if you come down that trail."

"You mean Bean Creek village?"

"Guess they call it Squawfield, don't they, over at Keene? Fellow named Ames has trading rights there."

"And that's your land?"

"It's part of it. And let me tell ye I aint plannin' on cuttin' down trees when I can plow that up first. Goin' to plow it this fall — put wheat in it. Ought to raise good wheat."

"Got any children, Maxon?"

"Nope! Azuby and me's alone out here. Got some grown children back east."

The woman sat on a stump and listened attentively to the conversation.

"You know you're in for trouble if you try to plow that land, don't you?"

"Used to it!" Maxon took out a plug of tobacco and bit off a chunk. After spitting, he continued: "Didn't I fight Injuns in the war? Fit Tecumseh's redskins right to the end — till the day they shot that red devil — and skinned him too, by cracky! Fellow in Ohio said he'd make drum heads of his hide. Said afterwards it made good heads — had a drum that beat as loud as any Injun could holler!" Maxon laughed in recollection of the past events.

"Guess there won't be much trouble," Maxon continued. "I'm used to Injun trouble. I'm a veteran, see. I'll just call out the army. The land's mine. I bought it! and they can get the hell off of it!"

"There are, however, Maxon, the rest of us to consider."

"Meaning?"

"The rest of us pioneers. Weve never had Indian trouble, and we don't want any."

"Then why don't we band together, Langdon, and drive 'em all out of here?"

Mrs. Maxon commented, "They've took 'em out of Indiana, why don't we send 'em packin' along with the others?"

"I don't believe it should be done." Martin thought a moment, and added, "Anyhow, I'd not be a party to trying it."

"I can handle it, if it comes to that. Hell, one white man's worth a dozen Injuns any day. You aint fit Injuns like I have. I've fit 'em from Detroit to the Thames, and I hate every Injun from hell to breakfast — men, women and papooses! Killin' Injuns has been my business, and I kin do it with a smile. Gettin' rid of Injun's the same as cleanin' out rattlesnakes — every dead one is one less!"

"Well and good if you're in the army, Maxon. But you're not in the army now. You're a pioneer — a settler, in southern Michigan."

"We'll get out the hull militia if we have to."

"On whose orders?" Martin's hand moved unconsciously toward the butt of his pistol.

Maxon's sharp eyes noticed the movement and he asked: "Afraid of Injuns, or aimin' to shoot honest settlers with that there pistol?"

"You know, Maxon, you don't ride around the woods with bears, wolves, wildcats and panthers, unarmed."

"And wild Injuns — don't forget them."

"How many settlers cabins have been burned here?"

"Can't rightly say."

"The only one I know of was my own, Maxon. And that was burned by a white man's order — by soldiers."

"For harborin' Injuns, I'll bet."

"Just a minute, Ed. I seem to remember somethin'," Mrs. Maxon got up from the stump. "Didn't you tell me that this man, Langdon, was hooked up with an Injun squaw?"

"Sure I did, Azuby. Claims he's married to her, and he don't want her moved west, with the other Injuns."

Martin restrained the anger that was welling up deep inside. The idea of Owaysa being moved west because she was part Indian was preposterous.

"It isn't that," he found himself saying. "These Indians aren't wild. They're peaceable – good neighbors."

"Don't you listen to him, Ed. If he's married to one of 'em, he's the same as an Injun himself."

"Get this straight, Langdon! I'm goin' to plow that field up come fall, if I have to set a torch to every bark shanty on it!"

Maxon took a step towards Martin, who held his ground and said doggedly: "I don't think so, Maxon. No! I don't believe you will."

"What you goin' to do about it?" Maxon's lips parted in an unpleasant grin.

"I don't know – yet!"

Martin mounted the sorrel gelding.

"No, Maxon, I don't know what *I'm* going to do about it, but I don't think you're going to like it."

Maxon lunged forward, reaching for the reins, but Martin wheeled the gelding quickly about as Maxon's voice rose loud and echoed in the forest: "I'll learn ye to talk that way to a man what fit fer the country, agin these Injuns!"

"So did my father!" Martin retorted. The gelding reared at a pull on the bit, and for a moment he wheeled him about and let him paw the air in the direction of Maxon and his wife, who drew back in alarm. Then Martin, suddenly letting up on the reins, galloped off in the direction of the Indian village.

II

The Smoke Rises From Many Chimneys

Martin's first impulse was to repeat exactly what Maxon had said, but as he rode through the village, past the dogs and children, he doubted the wisdom of a complete factual account, as he reached the chief's lodge.

"What Maxon say?" Baw Beese inquired.

As he dismounted Martin found himself in the midst of a gathering crowd of the villagers, and he made an attempt to seem composed.

"I couldn't get him to promise that he wouldn't plow up the land. He seems to think he has as much right to it as Bushnell had to Leathernose's cornfield."

"But Leathernose didn't live on the land as we do," Pamasaw objected. "This is our village and Charley Ames at Keene has the right to trade with us — from the government, he says."

"Possibly Ames could help you more than I can," said Martin. "If he's a trader with your village, the government must recognize the fact that you have a real village here."

The Indians were nodding in approval at this suggestion, when Kakatoma, breathless, and spent with running, limping and tired, made his way into the midst of the group.

"Me back!" he groaned, sinking onto the ground at the feet of Chief Baw Beese. "VanHoevenbergh behind in all places I go."

"Is he behind you now?" Martin demanded.

"Lost on trail. But he close, I bet."

"Ugh!" Chief Baw Beese was apprehensive, and spoke to Kakatoma in Potowatomi. The weary Indian reluctantly arose from the ground.

"Nagdoche-shaw!" Kakatoma was sullen.

"Martin," Pamasaw said. "I'm taking Kakatoma away to hide.

I could tell you where, but if you don't know, you won't have to lie. Hold the sheriff here for just a little while."

"If the sheriff comes, I have a job for him," Martin assured Pamasaw.

A horse was brought forward with only a rawhide bridle and no saddle. Kakatoma mounted, while Pamasaw's horse was being readied. No sooner had the young men left the camp, over a trail to the south, than Sheriff VanHoevenbergh, and a small posse, accompanied by Chee-chee-qua, appeared from the north.

"Well, well, Martin!" VanHoevenbergh greeted, without dismounting. "What are you doing here?"

"Oh, doing a little business," Martin answered.

Chee-chee-qua looked searchingly around the crowd of assembled braves.

"Not here!" Then looking straight at Martin she demanded: "Where is Kakatoma?"

"I don't know." And Martin was thankful that it was a perfectly truthful statement.

"None of these folks would tell us if they did know," VanHoevenbergh remarked.

"Look!" Chee-chee-qua took from her neck a string of glass beads. "Here's pretty beads from Frenchman. Me give anybody who tell where find Kakatoma."

Several of the women looked greedily at the beads, but no one spoke. Then, taking a large copper ring from her finger she held it up with the beads.

"I give this too!"

The sheriff, his posse and the Indian woman looked into every face in the crowd, but there was no response.

It was Martin, then, who spoke.

"There's more important business at hand right now than chasing Kakatoma."

"What's more important?" bristled VanHoevenbergh.

"Preventing the possibility of another killing," answered Martin.

"What are you talking about?" demanded the sheriff.

General interest was now evoked and lest his words might be misunderstood, Martin stepped close to VanHoevenbergh and said in an undertone, "A new settler here by the name of Maxon. Hates Indians on general principles worse than rattlesnakes. Says he's going to plow up this village if he has to burn the wigwams. There will be a general uprising of the Indians — Ed Maxon will be killed, unless . . . ."

"Can't have that happening," said the sheriff.

"What can you do?" asked Martin.

For an answer VanHoevenbergh turned to Chee-chee-qua. "You stay here, I have other business right now."

Chee-chee-qua screamed, "You know! You know! You know where Kakatoma be! I go."

Martin, mounting his horse, stilled her screams for the time being by saying, "We're going to see a man who'd kill an Indian before he'd hide him."

"Me go too?" Chief Baw Beese inquired.

"Just white men," answered the sheriff. "Come on men, we'll follow Martin." The Indians stood aside as they rode through.

When they reached their destination, Maxon, who was trying out his scythe on the long grass looked up in surprise. Seeing Martin who was in the lead he exclaimed somewhat rudely, "Oh, so it's you! Back again. Who's this?" pointing to the sheriff, and with a wave of his hand, "And all these other fellers?"

"Maxon, this is the sheriff of Hillsdale county, James VanHoevenbergh."

"Well, well; glad to meet yuh sheriff. May I have the honor?" He extended a somewhat dirty, sweaty hand to the sheriff who accepted it. "Might ye be lookin' fer stray Injuns?" he continued.

Before the sheriff could answer Martin interrupted. "I brought him over for you to tell him exactly what you told me."

Maxon acted puzzled, but with a somewhat crafty look in his eye and a voice which suddenly sounded far away, he posed the question, "What I told you?"

"Yes, you remember. Threats against the Indians. Just little things like plowing up their land, setting fire to their village. Go ahead Maxon, tell him!"

"Oh that!" But observing the sober reflection on the faces of the men, he passed it off with a shrug of his shoulders, laughed and explained casually, "Why I wuz only a sayin' I had a deed to that there land and seein's as how it's a right fertile field, it oughta be plowed up."

"And if you did just that and burned their village they'd scalp you. Maybe you'd like that!" declared VanHoevenbergh.

Losing none of his self-confident conceit, Maxon spat out his quid of tobacco and replied, "Well I wuz jus' talkin'. Didn't mean nothin'. Can't rightly say tho I'm scared o' redskins. I fit 'em in the war, back in '12 it wuz, and I've fit 'em from Detroit into Canada and..."

Sheriff VanHoevenbergh cut in, "But you don't 'fit' the Indians around here whether you own that land or not. Unless you have a court order to plow it up, you leave those Indians alone!"

"But I got rights, I have. You aint heered the last of it sheriff—not by a jug full!

"You heard me! Without a court order don't you plow up anything or set any fires. Hear me Maxon?"

"I hear ye."

"Then remember it! Because if you plow up that field without a court order and they scalp you, may God have mercy on your soul as the judge says when he decides there'll be a hanging."

"Gettin' a court order's easy. If that's the way you want it, that's the way we'll do it."

Maxon's wife, evidently tired from the labor of turning the grindstone had remained sprawled out on a nearby stump listening avidly to all the conversation that was carried on but now as the men wheeled their horses preparatory to leaving, she arose and running up to her husband whispered in his ear.

Maxon shouted, "Hey there wait a minute!"

VanHoevenbergh reined in his horse.

"Ben chasin' Injuns?" asked Maxon.

"Why?" questioned the sheriff.

"You didn't bring no posse out here just to see me."

"Well, I. . . ."

"Thought so," said Maxon slyly. "Well, jus' to keep the record straight on account I aint accused of obstructin' justice, two Injuns went off that-a-way on that there south trail on horseback just afore you come into the yard."

"Thanks," said the sheriff, and to the men he gave the order, "We'll go back to the village."

On their way back to Ko-jess-sug-wa-seepe, VanHoevenbergh inquired, "Did Kakatoma come this way, Martin?"

"I wouldn't know. He might have. But I'd say you've probably saved the lives of the settlers around here by heading off that fellow, Maxon."

"And in the meantime letting Kakatoma get another head start on me." VanHoevenbergh sounded irritated. "Are you sure you didn't see which way he went?"

"I honestly don't know," Martin answered. "Indians have a way of starting one way when you're watching them, then circling around and going in another direction when they're hiding in the forest."

"Oh I know, I know," the sheriff said wearily.

Martin knew that once again Kakatoma had escaped and the pursuit was beginning to be a futile task. He was correct in this conjecture, for when they returned to the village the sheriff told Chee-chee-qua that further search for Kakatoma was out of the question until such time as he might put in an appearance again.

* * * * *

It was Martin's secret hope that Kakatoma might have escaped to the land of the Chippewa, and when he was entrusted with the secret that such was the case by Pamasaw, he breathed freely after what had seemed an interminably long time.

Every day now, new settlers were coming in increasing numbers. Down the Maumee trail from the Chicago turnpike they were making their way. Loud were the sounds of their axes intermingled with squeals and grunts of pigs, the lowing of cattle and the bleating of sheep which more often than not drowned out the soft whisperings of the forest and the songs of birds.

And so it was that Chief Baw Beese asked of Martin one day, "Look – what you see?"

"I see the forest and my ripening grain."

"Up, far up the trail. What you see?"

"Well, I see the road which was once only the Maumee trail."

"Good! Now on road, what you see?"

"Nothing much but smoke from settler's chimneys."

"That's what we Injuns see. More here now than there are Indians. Pretty soon have no home left. Cut um down tree. No pay rent. Just say they own land."

Martin could not bring himself to explain to Baw Beese that the land was being divided without any just or honorable contracts whatsoever where the Indians were concerned. This was progress in a white man's world and if there was land that he wanted the Indian was expected to move elsewhere.

"Perhaps," Martin ventured, "the Indians ought to become farmers, tillers of the soil — that might solve his problems."

"But not like you, Martin! Not like settler." Baw Beese raised his arms, pointing to the horizon in all directions. "This is Injun's home! All outdoors! Sky, sun, moon — stars! Trees and forest! Injun no can live in little place like you. This place yours — all outdoors mine!"

"Well, if the Indians could farm land like the settlers, it would solve a lot of problems," Martin said. "Perhaps your young men could learn the art — keep livestock, and plant wheat."

Pamasaw, who was standing beside his father, proudly erect, silver bracelets on his arms, feathers in his hair, drew himself up and exclaimed, "Never! I am Pamasaw, son of my father, Baw Beese. My home is the woods — always the woods — for me and for my children after me." A sudden shadow suffused his features when he mentioned "children." Was he thinking of Wenojah, and the seeming hopelessness of his longing?

But even as he spoke a new family of settlers were putting in an appearance along the trail. They were coming in a wagon with a team of horses instead of an ox cart. Neither the man nor wife were youthful, for with them was a grown daughter. Her hair peeping from under a sunbonnet as she jumped from the wagon, was auburn.

The man and his daughter approached Martin, leaving the woman holding the reins of the team. "My name is Mergen!" The man extended his hand, "Anson Mergen! I have a claim out here!"

"Happy to meet you, Mr. Mergen," Martin was about to introduce him to Chief Baw Beese and Pamasaw, but the chief was drawing away, shaking his head. And Martin observed in that one brief moment the look that passed between the blue eyes of the girl in the sunbonnet and the brown eyes of Pamasaw.

12

Savage Meets With Savage

It was corn cutting time when Chief Baw Beese was visited by a rider who came to Ko-jess-sug-wa-seepe along the Maumee trail, bearing news of Kakatoma.

The Indian told the chief that he was sent as a messenger from the Chippewa to say they would have no part in the uprising that Kakatoma was planning.

"Kakatoma is like a man who is filled with firewater," said Chief Baw Beese.

"In our village we decided the same," said the Chippewa. "But he said you and your people would join him. Have you agreed?"

"I do not. The Three Council Fires combined cannot do what all the Indians under the great Tecumseh and the British could not do. We are at peace."

"It is as we thought. He's merely a boaster — he has no followers, then?"

"Not here," said Chief Baw Beese.

When the Chippewa had departed with the chief's message he turned to Pamasaw.

"This man," said Baw Beese to his son, "will surely get us into trouble. Go to my cousin, Moquago, and advise him of the matter."

As Pamasaw travelled along the trail, he stopped as though by accident at the clearing recently made by the Mergen family. That day he had met Betsey Mergen he had been strangely captivated by her blue eyes and auburn hair. The average person might have called her plain, and somewhat freckled. But she had a pleasant manner, and seemed thoroughly fascinated to meet a man she described in educated tones as a "denizen of the forest."

Pamasaw, for some reason, took this as a compliment, and had found it convenient to stop and see the Mergens more and more frequently, offering to help in cutting trees for their log cabin. At such times he sometimes saw Betsey alone. She had confided that she was engaged to be married, and he had told her of Wenojah and of his vow. But she had thought Wenojah ridiculous in her refusal to marry unless the settlers were driven out.

"She must be a very foolish girl to think that's possible," Betsey had said.

"She hasn't been much beyond her own village," Pamasaw apologized for her. "But I have been to Detroit, and once I travelled clear to the land of the Seneca in New York state."

Today, as he stopped at the Mergens, however, it was Anson Mergen who greeted him.

"About ready for the house raising," he said. "Suppose you folks will come and help won't you?"

Pamasaw smiled, and said he would bring plenty of help when Anson was ready.

"Betsey's planning on getting married," said Anson. "Want to have the house built, and have a nice little ceremony in my own little cabin, sort of a house warming."

"I see."

Pamasaw continued along the trail. So Betsey would soon be married. While he—well, at least he was on his way to see Wenojah and her father.

However, today, as he made his way toward Dry Prairie, he was taking neither his flute, nor a present. He was mounted on the very finest available horse and was dressed in his best buckskins.

On reaching the lodge of Moquago he found the chief was not there. Wenojah was assisting her mother in tanning a deer hide. It surprised him that he could address her in fluent Potowatomi in a bold fashion hitherto unknown to him. There was a feeling of finality as he started the conversation; for her consistent postponement of his suit had dulled the edge of his anticipation.

"Will the daughter of Moquago hear me today?"

He dismounted from his horse, and her mother conveniently absented herself; while Wenojah pretended to be intent on scraping the hide. She answered without looking up from her work.

"What does the son of Baw Beese wish to hear from the lips of the daughter of Moquago? Or is it that he just wants to tell me the moon is big and round at this time, or that the summer is waning, and that the leaves are falling early?"

"I want to know about Kakatoma."

"Kakatoma?" She pronounced the name self-consciously, and ceased her work. "Why do you think that Wenojah, the daughter of the great chief, Moquago, would know anything about a little chief like Kakatoma?"

"Have you promised to marry him?" he asked bluntly.

"How you talk, Pamasaw!" She dropped the scraping knife on the ground, and coming closer to him, patted the muzzle of his horse.

"You haven't answered me," Pamasaw said.

"You know my heart goes out to brave Indians — to great men!"

"And has he agreed to drive out the Long Knives?"

"Why do you ask that?" She continued nuzzling the horse, but her eyes studied him.

"Because he is making crazy talk in the land of the Chippewa. A man came to our village from Kalamazoo and wanted to know if it was true that my father expected the Three Council Fires to unite under Kakatoma and drive out the Long Knives."*

"And that is crazy talk, Pamasaw?"

She ceased her interest in the horse, and watching him closely, studied the expression on his face.

"Wenojah, if Kakatoma has told you he can unite the Three Council Fires and start us all on the warpath he is boasting of achievements he does not possess."

"He already has the promise of aid by many chiefs of the Ottawa and Chippewa," she asserted.

"And what of Pokagon?"

"I cannot say."

"I can, Wenojah. He has not seen Pokagon. He has only seen little chiefs, or more likely, just some men he has met in taverns." He was no longer the imploring suitor, and yet he was so close to Wenojah that he could have pulled her to him in an embrace. "He has no promises of help. We would be foolhardy indeed, with Long Knives all around us in great numbers. If Pontiac, Tecumseh and Black Hawk couldn't do it when there were fewer Long Knives than now, how could Kakatoma?"

* NOTE: The Three Council Fires, an alliance of Chippewa, Ottawa and Potowatomi which had formerly driven the Sioux, the Sauks and Foxes from southern Michigan.

"He has the promise of much help, I tell you!" Her eyes flashed defiance.

"If he thinks he can do it he is a fool. If we listen to Kakatoma we will all be killed — or worse — we'll be moved west of the Mississippi, into the land of the Sioux."

"It is not true! It is the Long Knives who will be going back to the land where the sun rises."

"And once your Kakatoma is caught by the sheriff of Branch county he will surely hang — or be shot."

"And will you, Pamasaw, tell where he hides so he may be placed in a paleface jail?"

Pamasaw hesitated a moment, and looked at the blue sky. A gray hawk was silently gliding above the green tops of the trees.

"Tell me, Wenojah," he asked, trying to keep a tone of anxiety from creeping into his voice. "Have you promised to marry him?"

"Only when the Long Knives are driven from our land." Wenojah looked at him defiantly.

"How could you have made Kakatoma the same promise you made me?" Pamasaw felt suddenly desolate. He could not keep the hurt out of his voice. "You said that your heart beat only for me, Wenojah."

"I've waited long for Pamasaw to show himself a leader of men — a great chief." Her voice was cool and soft, as though she were the one who felt neglected and alone. "I grow old — too old for marriage. Soon nobody but an old man will have me."

"And what does your father, the wise Moquago, say to his daughter promising herself to a man who has to keep himself in hiding from the Long Knives?"

"When the time comes my father will lead his warriors forth to follow Kakatoma."

"I can't believe it!" Pamasaw was silent for a moment. A red squirrel scolded them from a nearby tree. "No, I can't believe it — any more than I can believe the north wind will blow from the south, or that squirrel will snarl like a panther. Chief Moquago is a good and wise leader of men."

At this point Wenojah's mother came from the lodge and resumed work on the deerskin alone. The girl started to help her, but Pamasaw restrained her forcibly, drawing her suddenly towards him.

"And what of your manitou? What of mine?" he demanded. "I am to marry the daughter of a great chief who lives at a distance and you . . . ."

"I am never to marry until the Long Knives are gone." She wrenched herself free from his grasp. "Then I am to marry the man who leads our people to victory."

At this moment Chief Moquago himself appeared, carrying a dead turkey, which he threw on the ground at Wenojah's feet.

"Cook!" he ordered her. "We're having a feast in honor of the visit of the son of our cousin."

Wenojah gazed at the turkey which her father had thrown at her feet. The cooking would require a long time. She looked at her mother, who continued scraping the deerskin.

"Have I heard your daughter rightly, Chief Moquago, when she tells me that you will follow this fellow, Kakatoma, to battle the Long Knives?"

"The daughter of Moquago has spoken unwisely," the chief replied.

"If the Three Council Fires unite, and then ally themselves with the Miami to the south, the Kickipoo, the Sioux, the Sauks, Foxes and Cherokee — all of which is impossible — it would not stem the tide of the Long Knives."

Pamasaw spoke as one having authority, and like one of the old men and the wise men around the council fire, and Moquago looked thoughtfully at the young man. Then turning to his daughter he said: "You have spoken unwisely."

"I have done nothing wrong. If Pamasaw will not prove himself a brave man, why should I not tell him of Kakatoma?"

"Why indeed?" The chief stared at the turkey which still lay on the ground where he had tossed it. "Did the wife and daughter of Moquago not hear that we are to have a feast?"

Wenojah lowered her eyes, and looked at the dead bird. She picked it up dubiously, and inquired, "Shall I wrap it in clay and bake it in the fire, or put it in the kettle?"

"For a feast, it should be baked," said the chief.

The older woman discontinued working on the deerskin, and went with Wenojah to prepare the bird for baking. It would take a long time, and a great deal of mud and a big fire. For the bird must be encased in thick muddy clay before being baked in the fire itself, and when done, the clay must be broken so that the feathers and clay would come off the cooked turkey, leaving only the delicious meat exposed.

Pamasaw knew well the honor the chief was showing him by ordering a feast. He would like to decline the invitation since his courtship fared so poorly; but an opportunity did not present itself, until there was a trampling of horses on the trail.

Entering the village was the sheriff of Branch county, whom Pamasaw remembered as having appeared in Grannisville on the Fourth of July, with Chee-chee-qua. With him was a small posse.

After taking one look at Pamasaw, the sheriff inquired unceremoniously of Moquago: "Is this one Kakatoma?"

"He not Kakatoma," Moquago answered. "Why you think mebbe?"

"Well, I suppose you know we've been hearin' things about that Injun. They say he's tellin' around that he's the new Pontiac, and the successor to Tecumseh!"

"He's telling that, is he?" Pamasaw half asked and half stated. "Well, he's never told it to me."

"Then it's because he aint seen you. You're the only Injun he aint told it to." The sheriff turned to Moquago. "And we've heard too that he's back here with his own people after bein' up north for a spell. How's that, is he or aint he?"

"No see!" Moquago grunted morosely.

A sudden breeze sprung up. There was momentary silence, and the rustling of the leaves reminded Pamasaw of the time when Wenojah had called the sound the ghosts of Tecumseh's warriors, and he had called it the tread of advancing emigrants.

The sheriff, sitting motionless in his saddle listened too as though expecting a triumphant yell from Kakatoma and a following of painted braves. Then he turned to Moquago and said, "I think you're lyin'! You've seen him! He's back!"

"No! Choo-ween!" the chief grunted morosely.

"Mebbe not today! Mebbe not just now. I wouldn't expect an Injun to tell me the truth, nothin' but the truth, and the whole truth!"

"Neither today nor recently have I seen Kakatoma," Pamasaw came forward defiantly, the silver bracelets on his arms and the feathers in his hair in strong contrast to the carefully-worded language that he spoke.

"Who be you?"

"I am Pamasaw, son of Baw Beese, a great chief of the Huron-Potowatomi!"

"And what does the great chief Baw Beese think about this Injun?" There was some irony in the sheriff's tone.

"Who am I to say what my father thinks? But as to myself, if what you say is true I think Kakatoma's a great boaster."

"I guess we might as well mosey along, but we're goin' to keep an eye on this place. You stay here, Ed, and if he shows up, get word down to Branch."

"Not much I aint stayin' — leastwise not alone with these Injuns!" The man addressed as Ed looked defiantly at his superior. "That Kakatoma's run a knife in one man, and I don't figger on bein' the next one he tries it on!"

"See your point," said the sheriff. "Tell you what, Ed, suppose we go back to Holcomb's trading post and stay there awhile. Even if we caught him here might run into trouble, seein' we're in another county. Might run into the same thing we did with VanHoevenbergh over at Grannisville — he let him get away!"

The sheriff and his posse started back down the trail they had come, but even a casual observer would know they were becoming discouraged in their hunt.

Pamasaw watched the last of the horses out of sight before turning to Moquago.

"The Long Knives already know of Kakatoma's schemes. He is only succeeding in making trouble for us. It was bad enough that he should be wanted for murder. But to be hatching up a revolt as an eagle hatches its young, means trouble that we can't hope to face."

"Perhaps the Long Knives will never find him — perhaps they'll grow weary with searching."

"Then I shall find him, and punish him myself."

"What wrong has he done? He carried out the law of the knife and will be long remembered in the council fires of our tribe for the service he rendered us. Kakatoma is already a great man."

"I have my own score to settle, and it shall be in my own way. There will be no revolt, no warriors slain by useless battles with Long Knives when I find him."

"He is a strong man, Pamasaw. My daughter will become bereaved if her lover should be killed."

"I too am strong, Chief Moquago. Which of us will be mourned by Wenojah — Kakatoma or me?"

"He will surely prevail and she will mourn for you."

"It is no longer true. She has rejected me, in favor of Kakatoma."

"I find that hard to believe, Pamasaw."

"You said yourself he's already a hero among the people. Wenojah wants only a hero. She's made him the same promise she's made me — she'll marry him only when the Long Knives are driven out. No, Chief Moquago, Wenojah will not mourn for my loss. I can no longer consider myself her suitor."

"But you will think differently of this matter after the feast in your honor. Perhaps Wenojah will again smile on the son of my cousin Baw Beese."

But Wenojah did not smile at Pamasaw at the feast; and he remained unimpressed by the admiring glances of the other village maidens as they all partook of the roast turkey and sat around the glowing embers of the fire. Instead he found his hatred for Kakatoma increasing, and began to question in his own mind the promptings from his manitou that he was to marry the daughter of a great chief at a far distance from his own village.

13

The Savage Heart In Conflict

At Holcomb's trading post at Dry Prairie, Pamasaw recognized the man named Ed who was with the sheriff's posse. Pamasaw was on his return trip home, but he was in no great hurry. There was something dead inside of him. Something had gone out of his life, and left him desolate and alone. In the place where there had been love for Wenojah there was now jealousy and hatred for Kakatoma.

Kakatoma was his enemy — as much his personal enemy as any man had ever been. He felt that he had been robbed of something precious — something sacred and he must avenge himself for the loss.

He could tell the man named Ed that he too wanted to find Kakatoma, and perhaps even aid the Branch county sheriff in his search; but Pamasaw concluded, as he dismounted from his horse before the trading post, that his fight was purely personal. It would be something no one else could understand — least of all could it be understood by a *Ke-moke-mon.*

There was always gossip at a trading post, but the minute that Pamasaw stepped inside there was a hush, and he wondered if they had heard his secret thoughts, for all eyes were turned on him. There were only three people in the building — Holcomb, the sheriff's deputy, and an Indian whom he had never seen before, but all were intent on staring at him as he paused in the doorway.

"You Kakatoma?" Ed demanded bluntly.

"Of course not. You saw me a little while ago at Nottawa Seepe."

"Didn't get a good look at you. Anyhow you people all look so much alike to me I can't tell you apart."

It was the old familiar line of many of the *Ke-moke-mon* — if an Indian, no differentiation of character or features. If this be carried to the extreme of shooting first and then looking afterwards to see who was killed – well, Pamasaw certainly would not put this act past some of the settlers.

Holcomb did not know Pamasaw either, but he knew Kakatoma, at least he should have, because he had often traded with him.

"You want something?" Holcomb was not unpleasant, but his establishment was much like that of Charles Ames at Keene, and Pamasaw felt at ease in it, with its blankets, its cloth, and the smell of new things made somewhere by the palefaces. But Ames sold whiskey at Keene, and this was not in evidence at Holcomb's post.

"Yes," Pamasaw finally answered. "I'm looking for Kakatoma."

"Friend of his?" Holcomb inquired.

"Was once," Pamasaw looked into the face of the strange Indian who was watching him.

The Indian turned to Holcomb and said: "Him talk like *Ke-moke-mon!*"

"You from Hillsdale county?" Holcomb looked at Pamasaw.

"Son of Chief Baw Beese," Pamasaw answered. "I met you in the Swamp of the Skunk five years ago."

"A fellow named Martin Langdon was with you, wasn't he?"

"Yes! I went to school to him once. He taught me English."

"How is he, anyhow?"

"Oh, he's all right—likes farming better than teaching."

"And his wife. Did he marry that half-breed girl?"

Pamasaw's brow clouded momentarily, and he tried to prevent his voice from expressing the emotion he felt, when he answered: "He married Owaysa. They are in love—they are very lucky—more lucky than they know."

As Pamasaw stood silently looking around the room, his eyes staring in deep thought about his own love life, Holcomb wanted to know if Martin lived near the Indians, or in a cabin by himself.

"Oh he and Owaysa live in a log cabin. They have a cow and two horses."

"And his wife, how does she like being tied down to housework?"

"She is in love, and she is the sort that stays in love—with one man." He was trying to keep any trace of bitterness from his voice. "She acts just like a real settler's wife."

"Folks do funny things when they're in love," Holcomb observed.

"I'll say they do," said the sheriff's deputy. "I got a cousin—fell in love with an Injun, and up and married him. Lives over by Niles — with the Injuns!"

Pamasaw looked at the man named Ed.

"She changed like that?" He sounded unbelieving.

"She says she likes living with Injuns better than settlers. That Injun sure has some kind of power over her, I guess. We thought at first the fellow had used witchcraft on her."

"Well," Holcomb laughed. "Isn't being in love something like being bewitched?"

"Cal'late you're about right there, Holcomb. Come to think of it that's about the way we all act sometimes."

Pamasaw wanted to get away from this place. He wanted to think. This was a new idea—yes, he had been bewitched all this time by Wenojah. Her enticing lips, her eyes with the admiring glances, her graceful walk. She had bewitched him, and he knew it. Then the question of his manitou entered his mind. Could that too have been bewitched? Had a spell, such as Goon-pa-shee was said to be able to cast, been put upon him?

He suddenly realized that he must look very stupid standing there in the trading post, saying nothing.

"You say you're looking for Kakatoma too?" the man named Ed asked, bringing the conversation back to solid ground.

"Yes!"

"In on this scheme of his to fight us?"

"I am not that big a fool," Pamasaw answered. "Neither is my father. But I want to see him."

"Well, if you find him, tell him the sheriff of Branch county wants to see him too, will you?"

Pamasaw smiled and turned towards the door. "He already knows it, I'm sure."

Without further adieu he went outside, picked up the reins of his horse, and rode off down the trail which would take him to Grannisville. He would follow the Maumee trail all the way, and avoid the westward traffic of the Chicago Turnpike. Today he did not wish to meet the constant stream of emigrants in ox carts, covered wagons, buggies, accompanied by small flocks of sheep, squealing hogs, and maybe a cow or two, all interspersed with the "Tally-Ho" sound of the horns on the stagecoaches, demanding road room for their galloping teams of four or six.

On the trail that led from Kalamazoo to Maumee there were fewer emigrants and no stagecoaches such as thundered between Detroit and Chicago, frightening livestock, already travel-weary, and causing poultry to cackle loudly at the disturbance.

But now the only sounds along the trail were those made by the feet of his own horse, the song of a cardinal, a robin, or a thrush, sometimes interspersed with the raucous cries of a catbird or a bluejay. How long before this voice of nature would be only a dim-remembered yesterday? Then his mind again became disturbed and angry, recalling Wenojah's disloyalty.

The trail would lead him through Bushnell's newly-acquired field along the way—the field that had been in possession of Leathernose. Nobody knew how long Leathernose and his people before him had planted their corn, their beans, tobacco and pumpkins in that field. Now, by the motion of a quill pen by a *Ke-moke-mon* all his rights had been wiped out. No Indian would have questioned the right of Leathernose to plant his crops there, as he was, after all, the rightful owner.

This power of pen strokes to change the face of the earth was phenomenal. Fortunately for Pamasaw he could read what those pen strokes said, or could get a reasonable explanation of them from Martin. Other members of his race, however, who could not read, could barely get the connection between a stroke of the pen on a sheet of paper, and what happened later in consequence.

As he came to a glade along the way the strong fragrance of wild bergamot was mingled with the delicate scent of milkweed blossoms, and Pamasaw wondered if too, these sweet-smelling odors would be destroyed by the intrusion of the white man with his pen and paper instead of musket ball and hatchet.

Intuitively his hand felt of the hatchet carried at his waist. It was a pretty hatchet, decorated with the color from cranberries, elderberries and some stains from grasses and it bore very little resemblance to the article purchased at Morgan's store. And his knife too, another product from the store, with its stout blade and green handle, no Indian would rightfully know either where that had been made.

Time was, according to the old men, when hatchets and knives were made of stone by Pamasaw's own people. The bow and arrow, still used occasionally when the Indian was out of powder for his musket, also made by his people, was what a brave or a hunter used. But back before the days of even Tecumseh, the British had sold or given his people muskets and they had learned to shoot them. Few Indians indeed, could afford a beautiful rifle like Martin's, a weapon that could shoot game from afar off. Too many beaver pelts were needed which made the cost too high. And if measured in *shuniah* as the Indians called the white man's money, the cost of a rifle reached the unbelievable figure of a hundred dollars or more.

The world—Pamasaw's world—was changing so rapidly that it was confusing. He had been attempting to understand it—to face the difference in culture equipped with the knowledge of only his forest home and his people. He had watched with curiosity the strange ways of the settlers, and had been observing lately that they were relying more and more on *shuniah*, and less and less on an exchange of goods. If a settler wanted a blanket or some gunpowder he simply went in, placed *shuniah* on the counter and got it. His people traded pelts or baskets for the gunpowder, the blankets, knives or hatchets. They had little *shuniah*, which was the only thing the Long Knives would take when an Indian ordered whiskey. This was another mystifying thing, and as yet Pamasaw could only grasp a little as to the meaning or significance of money.

His father collected rent from some of the settlers, but many of them seemed to have little money also; and there were those who just laughed when his father asked for rent, saying they had "paid the government for land."

Another puzzling thing about money was the many different varieties. There was the bright, shining, golden kind, there was the white silver kind, and there was the copper color, not too highly prized. Then there was a sort of paper money that was sometimes used, but lately the Long Knives frowned on the paper money, speaking of it in the derisive terms of "Wildcat," and "Shinplasters." Pamasaw had observed these things as he had stood about in Morgan's store, or in the Great Sauk Inn at Grannisville.

At Keene, Charles Ames seemed to put a great deal more store on money from the Indians than he did on baskets, maple sugar, or other items of Indian manufacture. He kept insisting on *shuniah* and more *shuniah.*

The settlers seemed to get money from crops like wheat, and with it they paid debts, or spent it to buy more animals they were beginning to confine in open fields, where once the forests stood. They were pulling stumps from the ground with either horses or oxen, with log chains or big ropes, both of which sometimes broke. But in the end they all seemed to finish the year with some kind of money, instead of wheat, or corn, or other produce.

The only people who seemed to have an unending amount of money were the storekeepers like Ames or Morgan. They demanded cash or goods, and would even pay in money if an Indian had something they wanted and yet take nothing in trade.

Pamasaw's world was falling apart and he now realized it had been falling apart ever since he first saw Captain Moses Allen rebuild Campau's old trading post into a log house.

At first Pamasaw's people had laughed at Allen's ignorance on how to get along. He did not know anything about getting food from the forest itself. He did not know what was good to eat and what was not.

Then had come Thaddeus Wight, the first experienced farmer the Indians had ever seen, but even he did not know how to plant corn and beans, and the Indians had laughed at him. Instead of putting a fish in the ground, fastening it down with a pointed stick, and then planting corn, beans and pumpkins in the same hole, he did everything wrong by putting corn in without the fish and his beans and pumpkins separately. It was wrong but Mr. Wight had somehow been able to get a crop. But the strangest thing of all had been the plowing of the whole field with a metal piece fastened to a wooden slab, and then planting all of it to wheat. Finally, Pamasaw's people ceased to be amused, and just shrugged their shoulders. These were strange ways of doing things but they seemed to work.

Now the Indians realized that the Long Knives not only knew how to get along, but seemed to have a unique characteristic of acquiring an increasing amount of *shuniah* for their labors while the Indian, with much more land at his disposal had no more *shuniah* than before.

Today was the first time that Pamasaw had seriously questioned the length of time his people could continue in their old way of life. He had thought they could possibly retreat further and further into the forests, and at the same time exist as two different races on friendly terms.

This could be possible, but his people could no longer continue to live as they had before. They must learn to plant crops or run stores, but this they did not want to do. Pamasaw did not want to change. Why must it be thrust upon him?

He came to a rise in the ground that overlooked a gorge through which flowed leisurely a branch of the Sauk river, called the St. Joseph by the settlers. It moved lazily where once it proceeded rapidly because it was dammed up. The distant sound of the sawmill was another reminder, today. Even the forest was being eaten up—for boards, and chairs, and tables, were all being built from the trees. With the forests gone, Pamasaw and his people would either be forced into agriculture, or they would be forced into revolt.

Kakatoma had chosen to stir up a revolt—the worst possible thing to do at this time. Furthermore he had swept Pamasaw's world away when he had procured the promise from Wenojah that she would marry him. It did not matter that her promise had been the same to Kakatoma as to him. Of consequence was that Wenojah, whom he loved, did not love him for himself alone—nor did she love Kakatoma. She would marry *any* man who was brave, and could drive away the Long Knives, or never marry at all. At least she might have been true to him and not promise her hand to just anybody who would do her bidding. This made it impossible for him to believe longer in the dictates of his manitou, and that was the most confusing thing of all.

Even if he should find Kakatoma and prevail against him he could never again feel the same, nor could he trust his judgment or opinions with the same self-confidence or his little world with his idle boasting, his dreams.

His anger at Kakatoma continued to rise, and by the time he had reached the cabin of Martin and Owaysa he was in a savage rage, bent on vengeance. He was told on his arrival that Kakatoma had sought asylum which Martin had denied him, only a short time ago.

"He plans trouble, as my father has already spoken," said Pamasaw. "He has been to the chiefs of the Chippewa, and even more than that, to the village of Moquago and procured a promise from Wenojah."

They were standing at the front door of the cabin when Pamasaw was attracted by a movement behind an elderberry bush.

"There! There's Kakatoma now!" He quickly started toward the thick shrubbery, and Martin followed more leisurely.

"You are a boaster and a liar!" Pamasaw said in his native tongue.

"And you are a woman and a coward!" answered Kakatoma.

"You've boasted to Wenojah that you can get many warriors from the Chippewa and Ottowa, who will drive the Long Knives out!"

"That I can do, Pamasaw. I've killed one man who betrayed our people. Can you say the same?"

"You and your promises! Boastings to mislead Wenojah! The only chiefs who believe you are those in barrooms and taverns!"

"The son of Baw Beese forgets himself! He talks to a hero of the Huron-Potowatomi—one who makes his boasts, his deeds."

"Your deeds!" Pamasaw mocked. "And how far will you get with the Long Knives already knowing of your plans—and laughing, Kakatoma? Yes, laughing at you, and the Indians are laughing too!"

Like a panther Kakatoma sprang forward. Pamasaw sidestepped but with a sweeping backhand slap, Kakatoma felled him sprawling on the uneven ground. As he was slowly getting to his feet, and Kakatoma was pulling his knife, Martin stepped between the two and quickly twisted the knife from Kakatoma's hand. He threw it deep into a thicket.

"Now you get out of here and never come back!" commanded Martin. "And that's final Kakatoma! Do you understand?"

"Me show you, Langdon! Show all settlers some day!"

"I've a notion to turn you over to the sheriff now, and save trouble!"

By this time Pamasaw had regained his feet, and the matter was temporarily out of hand for Pamasaw fell on his adversary. This time it was Kakatoma who went down, flat on his back. But he was up in an instant and grasping Pamasaw around the waist flung him to the ground, but Pamasaw, wriggling free from his grasp, seized him around the waist and proceeded repeatedly to pound his body against the ground. Wrapping his legs around Pamasaw, Kakatoma pulled himself away, yanking the feathers from Pamasaw's hair, but Pamasaw, his hand on Kakatoma's throat, shutting off his wind, gave him a violent shove and forcing him to the ground, was drawing his knife, when again Martin intervened.

"Enough, Pamasaw!" he said.

"I kill!"

But Martin held his wrist, and said, "And have the sheriff after you? Indians can't kill Indians any more!"

Pamasaw's tense muscles relaxed and he permitted the panting Kakatoma to regain his feet.

"You go now," said Pamasaw. "The band of Baw Beese will never hide you again! Go to Chippewa — go anywhere, but put the space of many rivers between us."

Kakatoma smiled.

"I go, but not for long! I be back—with many Chippewa and Ottawa!"

14

A Church Service In The Tavern

Martin and Pamasaw watched Kakatoma swagger boastfully up the Maumee trail towards Hillsdale, and then turned to the cabin.

"He must be sure of himself, Pamasaw, or he would never have spoken those words in English."

"I don't believe many chiefs would follow him. The Chippewa and Ottawa are not losing their forests as my people are. Why should they listen to Kakatoma?"

Martin went thoughtfully to the wash basin. "He's hatching a plot," he said, wiping his hands on a towel that hung on a peg stuck into a log. "The sooner he's arrested by the sheriff of Branch county, the better—for everybody."

Pamasaw was silent, as he too washed his hands preparatory to staying for supper. He knew he was welcome although Owaysa had not asked him.

Owaysa set a place for Pamasaw and the three sat down at the table. Pamasaw watched his host and hostess use the silver knives and forks.

"These knives and forks," Martin said, "have just been sent to us by my father and mother back in York state."

Pamasaw smiled, and tried using the fork with its four sharp tines. Watching Owaysa, he spread his butter with the silver knife.

"It's possible," Pamasaw observed, "for one to learn to eat different foods, with salt in them, and in different ways than in my father's lodge."

"Well, I learned about big, wooden spoons one day when a certain girl offered me one." He smiled knowingly at Owaysa.

"And it's even possible to *like* food with salt," she said.

"Maybe my people could learn to be like the Long Knives—as you have, Owaysa.

"It's not been easy, Pamasaw. I doubt if I could have done it if I had not had a white mother. Like Martin she would never sit on the floor either and eat with a big wooden spoon. The Ke-mokemon will never substitute their mode of living which is far superior to that of the Indian, or so they believe."

"History proves it, too," said Martin.

"Then," said Pamasaw, "if I should meet a paleface girl, and we felt about each other as you and Owaysa, would I be the one who would have to adopt the white man's ways?"

"If you're thinking of Betsey Mergen, you'd better remember she's going to marry an old duffer from Adrian."

For a moment Pamasaw was self-consciously trying to get a piece of meat to stay on his fork with some beans, before he finally said in an embarrassed tone as though discovered in some depredation: "I know about Elihu Chapin."*

"So far as Betsey is concerned," Martin continued, "I daresay you both would undergo considerable changes. And what would be the reaction of your people to your plighted troth to Wenojah?"

"My people?" Pamasaw laid his knife and fork aside and studied the white panther skin stretched on the cabin wall.

"Yes, Pamasaw, our people need a leader," said Owaysa.

"They have my father," Pamasaw answered. "He's led them in war and in peace. They may not choose me as chief after him."

"But if they did—?" Owaysa persisted.

"Then I'll know what to do." Pamasaw smiled. "As it is now I don't know what tomorrow may bring. Either my manitou has led me in the wrong direction or I have misunderstood its meaning."

There was an anxious knock on the door, and the voice of Betsey Mergen asked: "May I come in?"

Without waiting for an answer, however, she burst into the room, red-faced and breathless. Pamasaw immediately stood erect and was staring at the somewhat disheveled, freckle-faced girl as though she had been conjured from his own thoughts and suddenly materialized before his eyes.

*NOTE: With apologies to Will Carleton and "Eliphalet Chapin's Wedding."

"My horse!" she gasped. "He's been stolen by that Indian Joe of yours!"

"Your horse?" Martin and Owaysa both asked simultaneously, Martin jumped to his feet.

"Yes!" she said. "I was coming back from Grannisville with some cloth for a dress. I stopped to pick some flowers and—and he snatched up the reins while my back was turned, jumped in the saddle and rode away to the north!"

"Kakatoma!" Pamasaw expostulated. "Now he's a horse thief!"

"Pa'll be furious!" Betsey said. "It'll be a wonder if he doesn't kill him!"

"We'll get your horse back for you," said Pamasaw.

Betsey looked at Pamasaw as though seeing him for the first time. "You — Pamasaw?"

For a moment he did not answer, as Betsey looked him in the eyes, and then turned demurely away.

"Yes, we'll get your horse for you," Pamasaw said huskily.

"But it isn't just the horse! I've lost the cloth I was bringing for trimming my wedding dress!"

"When's the wedding to be, Betsey?" Owaysa asked.

Betsey became self-conscious, and then spoke rapidly: "Pa says it'll be soon. Me, though—I don't feel much like getting married right now!"

"Of course not," Martin said. "But this misfortune will soon blow over."

"Oh it's not just that! If Pamasaw says he'll get the horse back he will. It's just that I'm in no hurry about getting married. Elihu isn't the type to make me want to hurry."

Betsey sank down onto a chair, and Pamasaw looked at Martin with an expression that said, "I told you so."

"Shall we go after the horse now, Pamasaw?" Martin asked.

"We couldn't catch him now," said the young Indian. "But my people will know where to look. As to the cloth, though—Idoubt if we'll be able to get it back."

"It was in the saddlebag," said Betsey. "It cost a pretty penny!"

"Well, we'll try to get it," said Pamasaw.

"Thank you, I know you will." Betsey arose, and turning to Pamasaw, continued. "It's getting dark, and I—I'd really like to have you walk home with me, Pamasaw, if you'd just as soon. It wouldn't surprise me if I met a bear, the way things are happening."

Pamasaw smiled, glad of the opportunity. "Bears can be bad," he said.

When the two left the cabin, Martin observed, "Strange goings on — in more ways than one."

"Yes," Owaysa agreed. "And they're not good things at all."

Martin went to the door as he heard a horse coming into the yard, and recognized Ed Maxon in blue jeans, a harried look on his face.

"You got to listen to me, Langdon!" He dismounted, tied the horse to a sapling and reached the door at a bound.

"Sure, Maxon, I'll listen to you! What's on your mind?"

Maxon looked over his shoulder suspiciously as though possible enemies lurked in the bushes.

"Talk better inside," he said.

Martin led him into the cabin and invited him to sit down. Owaysa continued with her household chores, paying little attention to their conversation at first.

"Now then," Maxon said. "You're so all fired sure these Injuns are all right, I've got something to tell you, Martin Langdon. I don't care if you *are* married to one of them."

"What have they done?"

"It ain't what they've done. It's what they're cookin' up!"

"You seem excited."

"Got a right to be. Know what? These infernal redskins is plannin' varmintry!"

"No!" Martin leaned against the mantle, and glanced at Owaysa who was now busying herself needlessly with minute details.

"Yes sirree! It's all over Grannisville and all over Hillsdale, or what there is of it. Heard all about it in Howder's tavern!"

"What did you hear?" Martin began filling his pipe. The one pioneer he had hoped would not learn of the plot knew it. Owaysa dropped a cup, but retrieved it without damage.

"This Kakatoma feller is plannin' a reg'l uprisin', that's what! You know, the feller what murdered the man over at Branch!"

"Of course, Maxon, there's a difference between planning something and doing it."

"Not too much with Injuns! It 'pears to me you don't know Injuns like I do!"

Owaysa dropped some knives and forks into the box where they were kept with a noise louder than necessary and turned angrily around, almost shouting: "Mr. Maxon! If Martin doesn't know Indians, who does? Certainly not you!"

Owaysa held a kitchen knife in her hand, and Maxon noticed it. He arose uneasily.

"Well, he ain't fit 'em like I have. I tell ye I've fit Injuns, and I know 'em!"

"That was a long time ago, Maxon." Martin took a long draw on his pipe and let smoke rings come from his mouth as he watched Owaysa with the knife in her hand. The expression in her eyes would seem to vindicate Maxon's beliefs. Martin made a signal to her with his eyes, indicating the kitchen knife. She appeared to have been unconscious she was holding it, and dropped it into the box where it belonged.

"Well, I vum!" said Maxon. "I thunk fer a minute your wife was goin' to spring on me."

Maxon walked to the door. "I'm callin' out the militia fer protection," he flung. Just thought you'd be interested in knowing what's going on. Because we'll all be back in the army soon's the fightin' starts!"

Martin closed the door and faced Maxon. "Just a minute! You're not calling out the militia! There's no need!"

"Stand aside, Langdon! I'm an old soldier and I know when Injuns is on the warpath! You and your kind will get us all massacreed!"

Martin looked at his rifle hanging over the fireplace, with the powder horn on a nail beside it. "That gun," he said, "will not be used against the Indians at Squawfield!"

"Wouldn't count on that, Langdon. "You'll take your little rifle where the Gov'nor tells ye! Besides that, I own Squawfield!"

"Got your court order yet?"

"No, but I'm goin' to Grannisville after it right now. I've put up with 'em as long as I'm goin' to do it. Last time old George Grannis talked me out of it. This time he ain't goin' to. Now let me out of here!"

As Maxon was mounting his horse he yelled, "And you ain't never seen the last of this yet!"

Martin made no answer as he watched him head north to Hillsdale and Grannisville. In the meantime Owaysa had stepped quietly to his side.

"Kakatoma's hatched a lot of trouble, my dear!"

"But Kakatoma is only an excuse Martin. Maxon is an evil man and he will cause trouble. I feel it in my heart."

"I know. Now I must turn the horses out to pasture."

Matters were coming more and more to a pass where the pioneers and the Indians could no longer trust one another. It was men like Maxon and Bushnell who were responsible. Settlers and Indians could live peaceably together if that was their desire. The government should not have given a deed to Maxon or anybody else for the land on which Squawfield was situated. Maxon had a legal point, and of course he could eventually win it. Martin hoped, however, that the militia would not be called again.

But it was not until a few weeks later at a church service in Howder's tavern in Hillsdale that the problem was forced into the open. It was the first service of its kind to be held in the village of Hillsdale, and the announcement had travelled over the countryside to the extent that almost every pioneer family was represented in the area.

The Rev. Darius Barker arrived on foot from Grannisville, where he served as minister of a pioneer church now established in the same little log building in which, several years before Martin had taught school for a time. The Pratts, the Mergens, the Fowlers, and even Maxon attended. Maxon, however, had not come to attend the service that afternoon. Instead he had come to get some help to dig potatoes.

"I haven't got time to dig all those potatoes alone," Maxon said. "It's time of year it's going to freeze up any day. Got to get some help."

"What about the Indians?" Mergen asked. "That's where I get help, when I want it."

"Sure, they'll be glad to help you," Pratt advised.

"Won't have the pesky redskins on my farm," answered Maxon. "Not if I lose every danged potato and I have to eat marsh hay."

It was at this point that Pamasaw arrived, along with Martin and Owaysa, and Betsey Mergen gave him an appraising glance; for Pamasaw, in his savage finery made a unique contrast to the pioneers and their plainly-dressed spouses. Now that the people were assembled they made their way upstairs following the innkeeper's order, and thus it was that the first church service in Hillsdale was held in the ballroom of Adam Howder's tavern.

This, however, was of little or no concern of Maxon's. He had come with one and only one idea in mind. There would be a lot of people whom he could contact all at once, so again he roared out as the congregation began seating themselves.

"I want to get a man to help me dig potatoes. Got too many to dig alone, and it's goin' to freeze up solid—feel it in my bones."

No one paid the slightest attention to Maxon's request and the Rev. Darius Barker pronounced solemnly from the Book of Common Prayer, "The Lord is in His Holy Temple. Let all the earth keep silence before Him."

Maxon looked around the room. All were very quiet and attentive. They knelt and they prayed in accordance with the service—all but Maxon who dismissed it as being just a lot of foolishness, until it came to the point where announcements were to be made, and then he arose, cleared his throat and pompously stated: "I'd like to announce that I want to hire some help! Come and see me after the service. I'll pay you for it."

"And what kind of help do you wish?" The Rev. Mr. Barker was evidently annoyed.

"Diggin' potatoes, that's what! Ought to be diggin' right now. Goin' to freeze up tomorrow!"

"Sh!" was the general sound around the room, and the service continued.

The sermon seemed especially suited to the occasion, since it was on the subject of change.

"Changes are occurring all around us every day," the minister stated. "There's something good in every change that comes into our lives, if we'll only look for it."

He outlined the changes that were transforming the forests into farms, that were taking place in the world, including the invention of the steamboat, and more recently the railroad, which he predicted would soon be chugging into towns like Hillsdale and Grannisville.

"Of course God never changes" the minister went on. "These changes are not made because God changed His ideas, but because man uses more and more of the ideas God has given him. We've discovered a new kind of government in less than a hundred years.

We've harnessed a steam teakettle, and made an engine of that steam that works for us. We've pressed forward into the wilderness building new homes where none existed, and starting shining, new cities. Of course we know they're not shining now, but they will in time, as man uses his God-given talents to accept the changes that are coming. And these forests of southern Michigan are changing too. Where once there were only trees, we now have fertile farms, more and more as time goes on.

"The Indians among us do not like these changes, but change will come, whether we like it or not. God has a plan for the world, and it is always for improvement—in better lives for all of us. And if we keep in mind that God's never-changing and ever-renewing ideas will see us through, we can accept these changes for the better.

"As the Bible tells us, the 'desert shall blossom as the rose'.

"We should never fight nor resist change, but let God help us find the good in it. We should help each change to become a step toward the better understanding of the working of God."

At the conclusion of the sermon the offering was taken. There was very little money, but all contributed something until they came to Pamasaw.

Martin knew he had no money. The young Indian stared at the tin plate that Adam Howder was passing. Slipping off a silver bracelet he dropped it in with the coins.

When the collection plate was passed in the row where Maxon was sitting he pretended not to see it, but after the singing of an old, familiar, hymn which concluded the service he turned to the group nearest to him and said: "I figger when I pay a man helpin' dig potatoes, I'm doin' the Lord's work too. Anyone comin' to help? It's sure as hell a goin' t' freeze!"

No one volunteered and Maxon finally stalked out of the room muttering profanity under his breath.

Before Pamasaw could leave, the Rev. Darius hurried to his side holding the silver bracelet in his hand.

"My dear man," he said addressing him, "this is worth more than all the coins on the plate. You may need it some day. As I said in my sermon, 'many changes are coming in these forests'."

"A gift," said Pamasaw standing taller than usual, "is a gift. I know the truth of what is to come. I do not make presents to people or to your God and then accept them back."

He turned haughtily away from the astonished minister and walked from the ballroom, his moccasined feet making no noise on the wooden floor.

It was a mild, beautiful day in early November, but that night it turned cold. On Monday morning the ground was frozen solid.

15

In Which Kakatoma's Plans Wax and Wane

When Kakatoma issued his parting threat to Pamasaw in Martin's field, he was aware that he could not carry it out. True there were Ottawa and Chippewa who would follow him, but Pamasaw had guessed the truth as to who they were.

They were of a low order. None of the great chiefs would even listen to his suggestions, pretending to a wisdom that old men assume. It was so obvious to Kakatoma that the old men did not know what they were doing that he marvelled that their followers adhered to them.

Any one could see with half an eye that the Indians were being crowded out of their forests by white invaders. The old men shrugged, smoked peace pipes with their leaders, some got drunk and signed treaties their tribal councils had prohibited.

But although Kakatoma could see that the old men had grown lazy he could not understand why more people did not follow the young men who were willing to risk all in an attempt to halt the tide of emigration.

"There are too many of them to even think of defeating them," Chief Pokagon had said when approached by one of the young men of his band. "The Long Knives have taken our country, and now we must abide by the matter, and get along with them—live with them."

Kakatoma doubted the sanity of Pokagon taking such a stand—not trying to stop the current, which was sweeping the people—the owners of all the forests, the lakes and the rivers, into an oblivion horrible to contemplate—into open fields where there would be no bear, no deer, nor even gray squirrels. The turkey was already getting harder and harder to find because of the insatiable hunger of the pioneers for the meat of the bird, and Indians were trading their kills for a very small amount of money, considering the increasing difficulties that had to be overcome to get one of them.

It was all very foolish and these troubles could all come to an end if it were not for the weak minds of the old men who were supposed to be wise. Kakatoma concluded, as he walked stealthily northward along the Maumee trail towards Grannisville.

He heard the galloping hooves of a solitary horse coming down the trail from the north, and he hid behind a tulip tree. When the rider came into view he could see that it was a woman—riding in a saddle as was the custom of the palefaces. He had never seen her before. She was alone. There were no cabins in sight. He could hit her over the head with his hatchet, and who would be the wiser? But one dead pale-face woman would serve no good purpose. He wanted a horse. He had to have a horse!

And then the opportunity presented itself. She suddenly drew in her reins and stopped only a few feet from the tulip tree, and began picking some big brown-eyed yellow daisies growing at the side of the trail. She dropped the reins and dismounted, and the animal was standing still.

As her back was turned and she was stooping to get the flowers, Kakatoma sprang into the saddle. The horse jumped high in the air, squealing at the force of the sudden impact of the unexpected burden on its back.

"Here, Bill!" she dropped the flowers and turned. Seeing the Indian on her mount she reached for the reins. Kakatoma grinned, deftly sliding along, as he bent over the saddle, and snatched the reins from her hands before she had a firm grasp on them.

"Here, you beast!" she screamed, "give me back my horse!"

For a moment she pounded against his leggings, and even pulled out a handful of the fringe. Kakatoma only laughed and the animal under his expert guidance and urging, dashed northward along the trail leaving the woman crying hysterically.

He had done well, but he knew that he must put many rivers between the spot where he had taken the horse, and his destination. It would be better to circle Hillsdale, but a horse in a forest was slower than a man, unless one could hit upon a deer trail. As for the woman—he'd never seen her before. A new settler, probably.

She might even blame that lazy old Baw Beese or his son, Pamasaw, for the theft.

Pamasaw! As Kakatoma thought of him he realized that something must be done. He was his enemy! If that treacherous Martin Langdon had not intervened he could have easily killed Pamasaw. He refused to admit that it was possibly Martin who had saved him from the knife of Pamasaw. Wenojah favored Kakatoma now, but again it was Pamasaw who made it difficult for him. He had had her father, Moquago, almost convinced that he should enter into no further alliances—now he could not really be relied on to assist him in carrying out his schemes. It was because Pamasaw had associated too long with Martin Langdon, and pretended to know too much. He was worse than the old chiefs, because he was young. His well-spoken English was bad—very bad. It gave him airs that no Indian had a right to possess. In fact, he was no better —even worse—than a Long Knife.

After circling Hillsdale, Kakatoma again hit the Maumee trail and rode hard towards Grannisville. Instead of turning west and going through Allen's Prairie, however, he followed the trail that led to Kalamazoo out of Grannisville. By now a river and several creeks lay between him and that screaming paleface woman. He felt an inward glow of satisfaction, but there was still a question of money.

The saddle could supply him with much-needed money, and he could probably trade it with Holcomb, whose trading post was too far away from Hillsdale to matter. Nobody there could identify it. He did not bother to circle the little settlement that was growing up around Bushnell's farm, but continued boldly along the trail which, with only a minor deviation, would lead him to Nottowa Seepe, and Wenojah.

Wenojah was the reward he was truly seeking—the prize for his bravery, his scheming and his plotting, an accomplishment he could actually hope to achieve only if successful. Still, she hated the Long Knives as did he. With Wenojah at his side he would feel confident enough to face even the Sioux if he had to. The Sioux were even worse than the Long Knives, it was said. They hated Kakatoma's people, as Kakatoma himself hated the *Ke-moke-mon.* But they never ended a man's life with a single shot from a musket, or an arrow, or even with a hangman's noose. When they captured a Potowatomi he was tortured to death.

Kakatoma thought it might be sport to torture people as the Sioux were reported to do. But somewhere along the line the Huron-Potowatomi had stopped practicing the art. This too, was another example of close association with the Long Knives.

He was only a little way north of Bushnells when darkness shrouded the trail in evening mists. The brilliant colorings of the autumn leaves were lost in shadows. The horse would have to stop and eat, and it would not be until early dawn that he would be able to arouse Holcomb at the trading post. If he pressed on, however, he might be able to spend the remainder of the night at Nottowa Seepe, near Wenojah. This, he decided to do, after letting the horse graze for awhile, and drink at a stream he was subsequently compelled to ford.

Eventually the moonlight revealed the trail more clearly and he could sometimes let the horse run. But the animal was spent and tired. He had travelled many miles, and crossed many rivers. Even Kakatoma could not force him to run for long, and it was nearly dawn when he arrived at Holcomb's trading post at Dry Prairie. There was no sign of life about the place but a couple of horses were browsing close by. With hobbles on them they could not go far.

Removing the saddle, he threw it on the porch, hobbled his own horse, and let him join the others as they fed on the aging autumnal grasses. Then he settled himself against a post on the primitive porch, and nodded, dreaming of a day when there would be again a free country. Perhaps, without even Holcomb's trading post at Dry Prairie. Perhaps his people would again take up their old ways of torture as the Sioux, the Black Feet and the Crows were still reported to do.

He was not aware that he was going to sleep, but he suddenly discovered that he had fallen from the porch on which he had been nodding. He was lying on the ground and big heavy bracelets were on his wrists. He had never known bracelets could be so heavy.

He opened his eyes and looked at them! They were iron! They were handcuffs! He rose up.

"Well, Kakatoma! Never figgered on getting you this easy," a harsh voice said, as Kakatoma sprang to his feet, raising his manacled hands high.

"Steady there, boy!" a voice behind him warned, and Kakatoma felt himself being held as in a vice of iron.

"Better put them handcuffs on over again, Ed. Put his hands behind him."

It was useless for Kakatoma to struggle. There were two of them, and no matter how he tried, he was unable to elude their grasp. His hands were forced behind him, and manacled.

"Where'd you get this horse and this saddle?" It was the voice of Fred Holcomb now.

The Indian refused to answer.

"Won't talk, huh? Well once we get you into jail my man you'll talk or you won't eat."

Kakatoma was unaware of the law which did not permit the sheriff of Branch county to arrest him in Calhoun county. But went silently off to jail with his captors, who roped his feet together around the horse's belly, and so in this manner was led without ceremony along the trail.

He felt as a bear on a leash must feel as he rode through the settlements, and was stared at by the women and children of the Long Knives, exactly as though he were some vicious beast. But he said nothing, and held his features frozen in stoical determination.

Never, no never, would he now abandon his plans—unless he were hanged or shot. Better to die in an attempt to free the people of these invaders than to live in such a way. The jail, built of logs, was small and constricted. This, above all else, he hated. He could not see the starlight at night, and the moon never shone either, just a trickle of moonlight making shadows from the bars on the windows. The autumn winds did not blow onto his cheek, chilling him in the knowledge that winter would be close at hand. A wolf, baying at the moon seemed farther away than ever before. The manacles on his wrists had been removed, but to be confined in the small space of a room of any kind was torture. It seemed like months before the prosecuting attorney finally came to see him. Actually it was only a few hours. With him was Chee-chee-qua.

When the door of the cell was opened and they stepped inside Chee-chee-qua looked at him in cold triumph.

"So," she said in Potowatomi, "the brave Kakatoma who stabs good people in the back is caught like a rabbit. The law is bigger than you, Kakatoma."

He looked at her defiantly.

"Speak English!" commanded the prosecuting attorney. "I want to know what's being said."

Chee-chee-qua smiled and repeated her words in English for the prosecutor, and Kakatoma's hatred for Chee-chee-qua flared even greater than his hatred for Pamasaw and the Long Knives.

"Besides this murder," the prosecutor said, "you've also been stirring up a revolt among the Indians—or trying to. What have you to say?"

Kakatoma continued to say nothing. He only stared defiantly at the prosecuting attorney, and refused to answer. He was so enraged at his helpless predicament that he could not talk if he tried. All his plans—all of them in ruins because he had slept when he should be awake.

"Not that your insurrection has mattered," the prosecutor continued, "because it hasn't. Even the Indians laughed at your foolishness. They weren't loyal to you. Where did you get the idea you could overthrow the United States of America?"

"He think he like Pontiac or Tecumseh!" Chee-chee-qua added insult to injury by spitting on Kakatoma's moccasins. "He couldn't find a single chief who'd follow him. Only crazy girl, Wenojah, listen—and she tell—she boast of Kakatoma! Ha!"

He would have liked more than anything else at that moment to choke Chee-chee-qua. She was worse than the prosecutor. But instead he only smiled—a smile he well knew would be more aggravating than an angry word.

"Well what charge shall I bring against you—murder or trying to stir up an insurrection?"

Kakatoma was not sure what an insurrection meant, but assumed it had something to do with his attempt to organize the Indians into resistance.

He admitted nothing, said nothing, and finally the pair left his cell and he was again alone with his thoughts.

* * * * *

Three days later Wenojah was permitted to visit him, but a burly deputy stood in the room with them, and they were forced to speak furtively lest some of the words be understood. But soon they realized he did not know their language at all, and Wenojah said boldly: "The horse you stole near Hillsdale—and the saddle. My father has seen that they were returned, as well as the paleface cloth in the saddlebag. It belongs to a sickly-looking red-headed girl who lives near Martin Langdon. Osseo, Owaysa's father, said that the girl's parents blamed it on the Indians around there."

"It was a good horse, fleet, like a deer," he said. "Is it true, Wenojah, that you boasted of our plans?"

"No, Kakatoma, I merely said that you were listening to the ghosts of Tecumseh's warriors—that you were a new Tecumseh—and a new Pontiac."

"That was how the Long Knives knew of my plans!"

"More than likely it was Pamasaw," said Wenojah. "He knew of your plans. His father, Baw Beese, knew of them. Perhaps they were the ones who told the Long Knives."

"I'd like to think it was Pamasaw! I hate him!"

"Pamasaw is young!" Wenojah answered. "His judgment is poor. He thinks the Long Knives cannot be driven away."

Kakatoma looked at the confines of his cell and wailed, "This is what the Long Knives offer us, Wenojah! Confinement in little rooms—the forest gone—our home destroyed to make way for the greed of farmers. And they would have us living in such places as this! I must get out of here! Get me out of here, Wenojah! I'll go to the land of the Chippewa. Not many Long Knives are there."

Wenojah shook her head. "I cannot get you out of here. I had to talk to many palefaces before I could even see you."

"But our plans for freedom from these people are ended," he said. "We are unable to push them back."

"Did you have the promise of enough warriors to achieve it, Kakatoma?"

He hesitated, and looked at her blankly. Her piercing gaze laid bare his soul, and he knew that lying would be useless.

"I had the promises of no great chiefs, and in fact, I had the promise of help from only a few little chiefs. I thought in time—they would follow."

He sank down onto the cot, which he rarely used, preferring the floor.

"Then there *are* no plans, and the Long Knives have nothing to fear?"

"I'm sorry, Wenojah. I had hoped to please you."

"But you've lied to me, Kakatoma. You said you had many chiefs who would follow. You said that Pamasaw was a woman!"

"No, you said he was. You would marry the man who'd drive the Long Knives from our country."

"And now where is the man I am to marry? He has never been born! I can never marry now! Better had you told the truth!"

Wenojah started for the door. As the guard was opening it, Kakatoma sprang to his feet.

"Don't say that, Wenojah! I can't lose you too! Then I lose all!"

"The daughter of Moquago marries only when the Long Knives are driven from our midst, Kakatoma, and she will marry on no other terms," she lifted her head proudly.

Kakatoma stared after her as the door of his cell closed behind her, then he pounded futilely with his bare fists against the log walls. He pounded until his knuckles bled.

16

Some Best Laid Plans Go Wrong

Because there was a great deal of unimproved land in Michigan, many pioneers never dreamed their squatters rights would be questioned. They hardly thought of themselves as squatters, but as settlers. Had they realized that much of the acreage south of the village of Hillsdale had been already purchased by Berton Lanman what happened in the winter of 1838 and '39 would never have transpired.

Martin and Owaysa, feeling secure in their holding granted by the largesse of Chief Baw Beese, came first to the realization that they had been too long negligent in filing their claim in the Monroe land office when a stranger, arriving in a buggy drove to their cabin door.

It was a mild day in early December, and although the air was crisp there was nothing to indicate the coldness of winter. Gray clouds scudded across the sky towards the northwest, driven by a strong southeast wind. The man, wearing a gray great-coat, topped by a tall gray hat, had a gray and grim look on his face, adorned by a graying beard.

He stepped out of his buggy and surveyed the cleared land, the cabin, and the small barn. Then he smiled icily, as he tied his horse to a sapling. Martin had hurried from the barn as he heard the approach of the buggy and was standing ready to greet the newcomer, but there was something sinister about the procedure that he could not quite understand. He waited for the man to approach him.

"Well, well," the stranger said. "Nice looking little set of buildings you have here."

"We like them." Martin looked around his holdings with an air of satisfaction.

"First time I've been out to see what I've bought," the man continued, as he approached Martin, who immediately became apprehensive. "Name's Lanman, Berton Lanman," the stranger continued, extending his hand. "You're Martin Langdon, I presume?"

Martin took the limp hand extended to him with some reservation. "Yes, I'm Martin Langdon. How did you know?"

"Found out who's living on my property, up at Howder's tavern."

"On *your* property?" Martin knew instantly what he was about to be told. He had been too late in filing his claim. But so had Pratt and the others. Only Mergen had been wiser.

"Yes, Mr. Langdon. I bought a thousand acres in here back in '34—just on speculation." He smiled icily. "Shall we go inside to talk it over?"

"I don't think so," said Martin. "My home is my castle, I believe."

"Not when I own it, Mr. Langdon. So let's go inside where we can talk things over and I'll explain it. After all you're only a squatter here and I have the deed."

Lanman started towards the door.

"I have my holdings here as a gift from the Indians," Martin said. "And I don't believe you bought this land in '34. It hadn't been opened up for sale."

"What difference does a year or two make? I own it now, and I won't be too hard to deal with."

"I'll need more proof than your word."

"Got it right here!" Lanman reached inside his great-coat and produced a deed. He waved it before Martin's face.

Reluctantly Martin opened the cabin door and let Lanman inside, saying, "This is my wife, Delia," as Owaysa came forward to meet the stranger.

"Happy to meet you, Mrs. Langdon." Lanman's sharp eyes scrutinized her closely.

"Mr. Lanman says he has a deed to our property," Martin explained.

"Then—" Owaysa's eyes were large, "it's true! What they say! They're selling our land without a treaty!"

Suddenly she stood stoically erect, her features frozen into a distant, haughty stare. She was motionless. Lanman seemed apprehensive.

"May I see your deed, Mr. Lanman?"

Lanman sat at the table without invitation, and warily spread out the deed. His hands grasped it tightly as he held the corners as though it might be snatched from him at any moment.

"There it is, Mr. Langdon. And it has the signature of Martin VanBuren himself."

Martin looked at the deed and could see that it not only covered his holdings but those of numerous other settlers, including Sam Pratt. "Well, I guess that proves it, Mr. Lanman. However, there are a number of improvements on the land, such as this cabin, my barn and quite a few acres of tillable soil that's all cleared of timber."

Lanman smiled. "Makes it worth more doesn't it. But I don't aim to rob anybody. Squatters rights are squatters rights, I say. Of course I ought to have a little on my investment, say twenty-five dollars an acre. That would be a fair price, would it not?"

"It only cost you a dollar and a quarter an acre."

"Well, of course that was on the whole thousand acres, Langdon. I was taking a chance—a thousand acres of unimproved land. And here I find it has been improved, already."

Martin paced the cabin floor. Owaysa pretended to be busy preparing a meal, but instead listened carefully as she placed a kettle on the crane in the fireplace.

"I'll give you just a dollar and a half an acre Lanman, and I want two hundred acres."

Lanman laughed unpleasantly, and began folding up the deed. "No, Langdon, it's no go. It'll be twenty-five dollars an acre, or I'll have you evicted."

Lanman got up to go and Martin asked, "Have you seen any other settlers here?"

"Not yet. This is my first call, but I'll be back in a couple of weeks, Langdon. Think it over. You have a nice place here. You're getting a bargain at twenty-five dollars an acre. I can sell it easily for that in Buffalo, sight unseen."

Lanman said no more, and went out the door, which Martin closed after him. Turning to Owaysa he said, "He's been here before. More than likely he knew the land was improved when he bought it."

"What are we going to do, Martin?"

"Well, we've been able to set aside a little money, but not that much."

"There's no way out for the Indian, and there's no way out of trouble for us, is there Martin?"

Owaysa sank onto a chair, and he stood behind her, his hands on her shoulders, his fingers toying idly with her dark hair she was wearing Indian style.

Finally he said, "Yes, Owaysa there's a way out for us. I wish it could be honorable, but maybe it can't be."

Her reaction was one of immediate fear. "The Indians? You mean using them for a white man's disappearance?"

"No, not that. Sam Pratt has already thought of that. A man can't just disappear any more. And I'd never think of laying it to the Indians. Remember Quaid, and the land he bought?"

Owaysa smiled in remembrance of the episode when she and her young husband had impersonated a panther in the night-time until poor Quaid, camping alone in the woods, had run for his life, never having been heard of in this part of the world since.

"Well, we can't scare this man that way, Martin."

"No, but there are other ways. We'll see what Pratt and the others think about it."

They did not have long to wait, for on the following day Pratt and three of the other settlers came to Martin's cabin.

"It's an outrage!" shouted Sam. "Twenty-five dollars an acre! He must think we're some of the rich Biddles in Philadelphia! The idea!"

"It's robbery!" said another. "I'm for tarrin' and featherin' him, and runnin' him out of the state."

"Now there," said Martin smiling, "is an idea!"

"But where we goin' to git the tar?"

"Maple sugar, boiled up. We'll get it from the Indians," said Martin.

"And feathers? Where in tarnation can we git enough feathers?"

"That does present a problem," said Martin. "Most likely though, we could get those too, from the Indians."

"We'll have to pay him something fer the land though. Hadn't we ought to?"

"I'm fer payin' him just his dollar and a quarter an acre. Git him to sign the deed first and then tar and feather him," said a settler named Bert.

"Say, Bert," said Sam Pratt. "I got a better idea. Why don't you just hitch your name onto the deed, and say your last name's the same as his, Bert Lanman?"

"Isn't much like Smith though, is it? What would Howder and those lawyers he's got up there say?"

"Well it's been done I've heard tell. And nobody ever did know what happened to the land grabber that tried it. They say the Injuns or a bear got him. That would be the best idea."

The pioneers sat on the freshly made bed, and on Martin's two chairs and waited for him to speak as he quietly and thoughtfully filled his pipe.

"Let's not talk of killing the man. He thinks he's made a slick deal no doubt. I presume he came out here, saw what land was improved, and then went down and filed a claim on it."

"That's just what he did," said Pratt. "I saw the deed. It wasn't signed until this last October. He came out this summer and figured it would be easy to make a lot of money on improved land."

"And of course the only settler here with sense enough to file his claim and make good his squatter's right was Mergen," said Martin.

"Where the devil could I rake up the money until I could get in a crop?" Pratt wanted to know. "That's why I didn't file. Why didn't you, Martin?"

"I guess I just never thought there was any hurry," he answered. "I've been living on land given to me as a wedding present by Chief Baw Beese and his band."

"Well one thing certain, we ain't any of us got a legal leg to stand on. So we got to use underhanded, tricky didoes to gain honest ends." It was Bert who spoke.

"Well we got as much right to be tricky as he has," said Pratt.

Martin said after deliberating for some time, "I'll tell you just what we'll do. When he comes again, you fellows all come down here. We'll set up a nice big kettle with maple sugar in it in a clearing in the woods, and we'll get the feathers if we can, and have them ready. Then we'll get him to sign that deed over to us, provided we pay him his dollar and a quarter an acre."

"But that would make a lot of deeds."

"No," said Martin. "The thousand acres will just be deeded to all of us at once, and then we divide it among ourselves later."

"He won't sign it."

"Oh yes, he'll sign it," Martin spoke with certainty. "We'll each be wearing pistols, and sort of scare him a little."

"It'll never stand up in court," said Bert.

"If we all stick together his word won't be worth much in this part of the country," said Martin. Besides that, don't forget the feathers... he'll leave here well-sweetened, and with more feathers than just a feather in his cap and in his own buggy."

"Danged if you ain't right, Martin."

"Now the question is, can we raise between us the twelve hundred and fifty dollars to pay him for the land."

They all looked at one another and then began counting on their fingers.

Between the entire group it was finally agreed that they could raise about twelve hundred dollars.

"I'll sell the bald-faced mare," said Martin. "That'll make up the difference."

"Martin!" Owaysa interrupted. "Not her! She's the first horse we had. She was a present to us!"

"We have to get fifty dollars more somewhere, Owaysa."

"Borrow it from Baw Beese," she said brightly.

The pioneers all looked at her in surprise.

"I mean it," she said. "Chief Baw Beese wants us to have this place. He'll be glad to help us keep it."

And so after reluctant consideration of the question at hand, the men agreed to delegate to Martin the worry of raising another fifty dollars from the Indians.

It was with some misgivings that Martin, saddling the gelding rode off on the next crisp December morning to Squawfield to lay his plea before the Indian chief who had done so much already for the pioneers, often providing them with food, and even medicine.

Martin first explained to the chief, whom he found at home in his lodge, the plight of the settlers, and the plans about the maple syrup and the feathers.

Chief Baw Beese laughed long and hard at the suggestion of dealing with the "city slicker" out to beat the pioneers. He agreed that there would be plenty of feathers available to the pioneers, and would permit the use of a big copper kettle for the occasion as well as supplying enough maple sugar to make a thick mixture. But as to the money needed he was dubious. He would have to confer with others.

It was not until Martin had returned home that Pamasaw arrived with the news that he himself would like to own some land. He would procure the needed fifty dollars, he said.

"But that means you're buying your own property," said Martin.

"I want a deed to it, the same as Maxon who says he has a deed, and I will sell my horse."

"But Pamasaw," Owaysa said. "Your fifty dollars will not buy you the great, big, wonderful out-doors which is yours now—only a very small plot which when measured out is very little land."

He smiled. "I know, but not even the *Ke-moke-mon* can take it away from me, then."

Martin grinned, and inquired, "What would you do with it, Pamasaw?"

"Build a bark house on it, and keep everybody off the land but Indians," he answered.

"Well," Martin was dubious about accepting such an offer. "I don't know about that. When we deed the land it'll seem odd to read the name Pamasaw on it."

"My name means Flying Bird," he answered. "All the settlers call Indians 'Bill' or 'Joe'. Now a blue jay is a bird. I've thought it over before. I'll be known as Joe Jay."

Owaysa looked at him in astonishment.

"Jays are noisy and quarrelsome," she said. "I don't think it's a good name for you."

"It'll do on a deed. Aren't there any white men named Jay?"

Martin remembered the historic name of John Jay, who had made the treaty with England in which the United States finally was given the city of Detroit, and with it the Northwest Territory.

"Yes, Pamasaw, there was once a very famous man, named John Jay, a friend of President Washington. Why not use that name?"

"Yes, that shall be my name on the deed! I like that name 'John Jay' better. Sometimes Indians are also called 'John'."

More to humor his young friend than because he believed the deed would actually mean anything to him, Martin agreed that he would see, when the time came, that his share of the acreage worth fifty dollars, would be deeded to him as John Jay.

"Good," said Pamasaw. "Now I'll go to Hillsdale or Grannisville and offer my horse for sale."

When he had gone Owaysa said to Martin, "That is the most useless thing I've ever heard of Pamasaw doing. Whatever does he want with a deed? And why should he choose a name like John Jay?"

"Well, Owaysa, if you don't know, who would?" He looked at her thoughtfully a moment. "I have an idea, if you haven't. He's going to build a house on it, he said."

"You mean . . . ?"

"Yes. It's my guess he's thinking of Betsey Mergen."

"And what of his vow and Wenojah—and his marrying the daughter of a great chief born a distance from his village?"

"His vow doesn't have to include Wenojah. Who knows—maybe Anson Mergen was a great chief—back east?"

"But Anson Mergen isn't an Indian, Martin."

"I know; they don't call the very important people of the white race, 'chiefs'—sometimes just 'Mister" and bow down to them very humbly as you do to me," he teased. Then going over to her where she was standing by the hearth, he took her in his arms, kissed her and added, "as for you, my beautiful young lady, to me, you will always remain my very lovely Princess."

17

Some Legal Rights Are Fairly Won

Of all the settlers south of Hillsdale, it seemed that Anson Mergen alone was the only one who did not come frequently to Martin's cabin to talk over the impending arrival of Berton Lanman, and the manner in which they were to deal with him.

The maple sugar was stored in Martin's barn, along with a big copper kettle borrowed from the Indians. A quantity of wood was assembled at the clearing in the forest where Owaysa had been communing last summer with her manitou.

But the feathers provided by the Indians were too few.

"Tell you what," said Sam Pratt. "We brought a feather tick with us, and it got all wet before we got our cabin built. Then it got mildew in it, and that will supply more than enough feathers to really do a good job."

So the feather tick was also brought to Martin's barn.

"Now as to this money," Sam Pratt asked, "Have we all got it?"

Martin said that he had his, and that his Indian friend Pamasaw would put in for part of the land.

"Pamasaw?" the man named Bert, but no relation to Lanman was perplexed. "What's that Injun going to do with land? Hasn't he got enough?"

"He says he wants a white man's deed."

"But Pamasaw. How'll that look on a deed?"

Martin explained that the name to be added to the deed would be John Jay, so all were in accord to let the young Indian in on the scheme. To further define Pamasaw's desire Martin said, "He wants fifty dollars worth of land adjoining Panther Lake."

The pioneers agreed that this too, would be satisfactory and began planning on how the division of the thousand acres of land would be assigned when the deed was once in their possession.

Martin, they decided, since he had been a former school teacher, should be a trustee, and that he draw up a document to that effect. This done, they all signed a paper and took it to Hillsdale, where they had the lawyer, James Kinman, notarize it.

"I feel better now that it's all legal," said Sam Pratt. "Nobody's going to take unfair advantage under this law. Even that lawyer said the agreement was legal."

"Of course what we failed to mention," Martin said, "was that we don't have the deed to the land in our possession yet."

"No, but we're sort of a company—a land company now, and what he doesn't know won't hurt him."

"But it's going to hurt Mr. Lanman. He's so sure of getting a lot of improved land, ready to sell other pioneers at a big profit."

"Let him try it," was the boast.

Then they waited for the appearance of Berton Lanman in the neighborhood. Their transaction had been completed well ahead of the two weeks he was alloting to them to raise the twenty-five dollars an acre. But Lanman did not appear.

Day after day they waited for the return of the land-shark and there was no sign of him. The crisp air of early December turned to bleak ice and snow. Christmas came and went, and there was still no sign of Lanman.

The snows of January had buried the pile of wood the pioneers had prepared to melt the maple sugar into syrup for what they called the "tar and feathering." The feather tick lay waiting the event in the barn, and the big copper kettle had gathered a quantity of chaff from the hay as Martin brought it in from the out door haystack.

The settlers were cognizant of every movement along the snowy trail that was turning into a road. No strangers traversed it south of Hillsdale. The only white man not an integral part of their neighborhood who made infrequent trips for supplies was Maxon, and he never stopped to pass the time of day with Martin, but did speak when he met him face to face.

Ond day in early February he said as he met Martin along the road, "I've writ the president about them Injuns on my property."

"And what did the President say?" Martin asked.

"Ain't said nothin' yet. But he will."

But the pioneers were not immediately concerned about Maxon and his letter writing. Pamasaw said that he had heard that Kakatome was still in jail in Coldwater, and that the prosecuting attorney was awaiting word from Governor Mason as to what to do with him. So far as he had been able to determine the governor had only written back that he was "considering the matter closely."

The Indians, Pamasaw said, were highly resentful that Kakatoma should be in jail, but had no interest in his plans for starting an insurrection. As to Wenojah, he had also learned she was continuing her visits to him in jail. Once he mentioned rather sadly that Betsey Mergen was planning on getting married when the spring thaws came.

"You've known all the time she's to marry Elihu Chapin! Does it bother you?"

"Well, I don't think she wants to marry him."

"Of course she can't marry you," Martin said.

"Because I'm an Indian?"

"For one thing there's your manitou to consider. You once told me you couldn't go against the prophetic omens you received from your manitou."

Pamasaw did not answer, and continued on his way down the trail toward Ko-jess-sug-wa-seepe. But Martin had the idea that he would probably stop in at the Mergens.

It was in early February, and the promised visit of Lanman had not materialized. The settlers knew he would be back some time, and were getting somewhat jittery. The snows had halted the tide of migration but now the carefully prepared woodpile was covered with a layer of ice that had followed the customary January thaw. Surely Lanman would be coming any day, and the delay was beginning to tell on their nerves. For the most part they were men of action. When a plan was made it was carried out forthwith. Careful plans such as theirs were not to be delayed. Their future homes were at stake, and had they known where to locate him they would have searched him out in a body. In fact, that idea was suggested, but they realized they had not the faintest notion where his home could be. Furthermore, if found, they might not be able to carry out their plan successfully. So they continued to await his coming with what patience they could summon, frequently gathering at Martin's cabin, and talking of the crops they were putting in when spring came, how much of the forest they had cut during the winter, and how much lumber they could dispose of at the saw mill. Lumber was not in great demand, and Anson Mergen, who seemed to have the extra cash took enough whitewood logs from his place to the Cook and Ferris saw-mill at Hillsdale, to furnish the material needed for a frame house.

It was easy to pull logs on a big sled over the frozen terrain, and one day as he was hauling a load of sawed lumber home he stopped in at Martin's to warm himself at the fireside.

"I sort of hoped to have a new house come fall," he said. "But after all with Betsey getting married this spring, I don't know what my wife and I'll need of a new house."

"Hope to have one myself some day," said Martin.

They sat in the small cabin, and Owaysa was about to place some wood on the fire, when she apparently grew faint, and grasped the mantle for support. Martin jumped out of his chair and went over to her.

"What's the matter, Owaysa?"

She smiled and said, "I don't know. I guess I just felt dizzy, as though I might faint." Then she straightened up proudly. "Only weaklings do that, don't they, Mr. Mergen?"

"I wouldn't say so," Mergen remarked. "Most women do, I calc'late, at one time or another." He paused and looked wisely at Martin. "This be your first child?"

Martin was surprised, and showed it. He looked at Owaysa in wonder, and she smiled self-consciously, but accepted his offer of assistance to a chair. It was she who answered, "Yes, it will be our first child."

"They say the first one is the worst," he said. "But I wouldn't know. We have only Betsey, who will soon have her own home. I'll be on my way now, thanks for your hospitality and warm fire," and turning to Owaysa patted her on the shoulder and said, "Now don't you have any worries about being a weakling."

Martin was too surprised by Owaysa's revelation to even say good-bye as Anson left the cabin, but when the door closed he lifted her to her feet and took her tenderly in his arms.

* * * * *

It was not until the last week in February that any of the pioneers heard again from Berton Lanman. One of them had reported that he was seen in Grannisville at the Great Sauk Inn.

"Didn't know me," said Sam Pratt. "But I heard him tell he had a thousand acres of land south of Hillsdale, and he was goin' to make a killin' on his money."

"Much of an audience?" Martin inquired.

"Well, tolerable, I'd say. But mostly folks that didn't take kindly to such boasts."

"Good," said Martin. "When's he coming to take over?"

"Didn't stay to find out, but it'll be right soon, I calc'late."

And so it was. The following day with sleigh-bells softly jingling through the keen, frosty air, a horse-driven sleigh came down the Maumee trail and stopped at Martin's cabin. He opened the door after the heavy knock which seemed to even shake the rafters. Lanman had used the butt end of his whip to rap on the door. Lanman was dressed for the cold weather with his great-coat topped by a muffler and the ear-flaps of his fur cap turned down.

"Well, Mr. Langdon, I've given you plenty of time to think over my little proposition," he began without the formality of a greeting. "In other words I've come to collect."

"I've expected you before this," Martin said. "Won't you come in?"

Lanman came pompously into the cabin stamping the snow from his feet onto the puncheon floor. He studied Martin's features as though curious about the cordiality he was expressing.

"How much land are you going to take, Mr. Langdon?"

"Why my friends and I are going to take it all, Mr. Lanman."

Martin sat down in a chair, and began filling his pipe. He seemed about to say more, but waited for Lanman.

"You mean you'll take the whole thousand acres at twenty-five dollars an acre?"

"I didn't say that."

"That's the going price, Langdon." Lanman scowled.

"I said we'll buy the whole thousand acres."

"For how much?"

Martin lit his pipe leisurely and blew several smoke rings before answering.

"Not just what you're asking, Lanman. We settlers are a wee might hard to deal with at your price."

"I don't figure on cutting the price—not much I don't. It's twenty-five dollars an acre, cash on the line or out you go—the whole kit and caboodle of you!"

Martin watched Lanman as he stood defiantly near the door when suddenly it opened and Pamasaw glided in. Lanman gave way slightly to the young Indian and Martin stood up.

"Pamasaw, this is Mr. Berton Lanman," he said. "I think you'd better tell Sam Pratt and some of the others that he wants his money."

"You just betcher life I do," Lanman said.

Pamasaw, saying nothing, quietly went out the door as silently as he had entered.

Owaysa, who had been sitting by the fireplace working out an intricate pattern on a pair of tiny deer-skin moccasins, remembered her manners and asked their uninvited guest to sit down.

Lanman looked around the cabin with its homemade furniture. Then, looking suspiciously at Owaysa, replied, "No thanks, I'll stand. Feel safer standing up."

"It won't be long, Lanman. Pamasaw'll soon be back with—"

"With who, Langdon?" he asked, suddenly alerted and wary.

"Some friends of mine."

"You mean Injuns?"

"What's the matter, Lanman. You aren't afraid are you?" Martin held his pipe in his hand and smiled.

"There's something danged funny going on here. Maybe I ought to leave, and come back with eviction orders." He turned, but Martin bounded to his feet and barred the doorway.

"No, Lanman, you're going to stay here!"

"Get out of my way, you... you... I'll——" Lanman took a step forward, and then thinking better of what he had in mind, hesitated as Martin coolly addressed him.

"You'll surely want to wait to hear our proposition. You've come out here to get some improved land—cheap! We've done the work, and you get the profit. Now we're going to buy it of you."

"For twenty-five dollars an acre! You fellows got that kind of money?"

Martin said nothing, but remained in front of the door. Outside the sleighbells jingled gently as the horse pawed restlessly in the frozen snow.

Lanman hesitated a moment, then relaxed, but remained silent. Owaysa, placing her work aside replenished the fire by noisily adding another log. Then she went to the mantle, and procuring Martin's pistol, walked across the room and presented it to him, butt first.

"It's loaded Martin," she remarked, and going back to her seat by the fireside concentrated once more on the tiny moccasins.

Lanman's easy manner left him. He stood motionless, his gaze alternating between Martin's face and the pistol he held loosely in his hand. Finally he found his voice.

"See here, Langdon, if you think you can threaten me, remember I don't scare." His voice, however, belied the words.

Martin remained silent, and continued barring the way to the door. But he knew that Lanman was very much afraid, and that predicated well for the scheme as planned.

Nothing more was said until about five minutes later the sound of footsteps was heard in the snow. Lanman paled when the door opened and several settlers entered noisily, all with muskets in their hands.

Lanman's face turned from pale to ashen. "What—what do you men intend to do?" he demanded.

"Mr. Lanman, we're going to buy your thousand acres," Sam Pratt said.

"For the same price you paid for it—a dollar and twenty-five cents an acre," Martin delivered the ultimatum in a cold voice.

"But— but—"

"Quite a few fellows like you come up missing in the woods," Sam Pratt remarked.

"Going to threaten me, are you? Well, let me tell you something. Everybody in Hillsdale knows where I am and why."

"Oh, we haven't the slightest doubt of that, Lanman," Martin said. "Now if you'll just sign this deed we'll let you go back to Hillsdale."

Martin spread the deed out on the table.

"I won't do it!"

"Mebbe tar and feathers'll make you think different," the pioneer named Bert said.

"You wouldn't dare!" Lanman's features showed mingled rage and awe as he looked around the room. Pamasaw entered the cabin, his knife in his hand, at that precise moment, and Lanman stepped over to the table, looking at the paper Martin had spread out.

"It's not legal!" Lanman said. "If you fellows force me to sign that paper I'll have the law on you!"

"All right, let's take him to the woods!" Martin said. And without further words, the pioneers hustled the sputtering land shark out the cabin door. They stopped at the barn to pull out the maple sugar, and the discarded feather tick.

"I'll have the law on you for this!" Lanman shouted.

"Keep yelling," Sam Pratt said. "Nobody's going to hear you out here!"

When they reached the clearing the snow was pulled off the copper kettle, and some dry sticks from the bottom of the wood pile were unearthed. With flint and tinder a blazine fire was soon burning and the maple sugar was dumped into the huge cooking vessel.

"That isn't tar!" Lanman finally managed to say. "It smells like maple syrup."

"It is maple syrup!" Martin said. "Too sweet for you, but we hope you don't mind. It'll all serve the same purpose."

"Easy on the water!" ordered the man named Bert. "The syrup's got to be thick, you know."

"And it will be boiling now pretty quick, so I'll get the feathers ready," and taking out his knife, Sam Pratt slit open the mildewed tick.

"Well, Lanman, better start undressing," ordered Martin in a most business-like tone of voice.

"The hell I will!" Lanman shouted. "Think I'm a tool?"

"No!" Martin looked at him. "I think you're a calculating rascal. You're just lucky. We've heard of many a man like you who went to claim his land and was never heard of again."

"Sure are lucky, Lanman! In addition to a coat of feathers we're also giving you a free ride on a pole—haven't got any rails around here," spoke up another voice.

"But the sleigh! The horse!" Lanman moaned. "You'll get in plenty of trouble over the horse."

"Oh, he'll turn up all right. You rented him, didn't you?"

Lanman refused to answer.

"I'll have my wife drive the horse back," said Martin. "Come,

Lanman, the maple syrup is just about ready! Get your clothes off, or do you want us to take them off for you?"

Lanman stepped away, but Martin took him roughly by the arm, and half turning him around pushed him into the arms of Sam Pratt and Pamasaw.

"Calc'late he wants us to undress him!" Sam yanked off Lanman's cap, and Pamasaw snatched away his scarf.

"No! No!" wailed Lanman. "Please—please don't!"

The man named Bert guffawed, and the others laughed. "Please—please, Mr. Lanman! Won't you give us back the land we've worked?" he mimicked.

"I came by it honestly!" Lanman barked.

"You came by it after you saw it was all improved, then you went down to the land office and grabbed it," said Martin. "You were out here and looked it all over beforehand."

"I'll let you have it for ten dollars an acre; and now let me go." Lanman looked furtively at the kettle.

"Come, come, you're wasting time." Martin was impatient. "Take off his great coat, Bert!"

It took two men to hold him, but Bert deftly unbuttoned the heavy coat. Shaken and furious he stood before them in his tail coat and pantaloons. His teeth began to chatter.

"I'll deed you what land you can pay for at five dollars an—an acre." His eyes looked from one to the other.

But the pioneers were obdurate.

"Now his bee-utiful plum-colored coat and that fancy waistcoat," purred Sam, snatching off the coat quickly as Martin started undoing the buttons on the waistcoat.

"No! No! No!" Lanman shouted "Dammit to hell! Hand over your lousy old paper if you want me to sign it!"

"What do you say, boys?" Martin looked at the others.

Lanman in his shirt sleeves was obviously cold, but he was also badly frightened, however hard he tried to conceal it.

"We ought to tar and feather him, or maple sugar him anyhow, so long as we've gone this far," said Pratt.

"Yes!" Pamasaw smiled.

"Come on, Lanman, the shirt is next, and then the pantaloons!"

"No! No! That hot syrup'll scald me! I've told you I'd sign you the land!"

"And then have us all arrested. We're onto that one, Lanman!" Martin strode over to the kettle and looked in. Turning to the others he said, "Well, it's just about ready. That's a nice pile of feathers! Will there be enough?"

"With what the Indians have given us there's more than plenty for the job," said Pratt. "Come on Lanman, get off your shirt!"

"What do you fellows want?" Lanman's bravado forsook him and his voice quivered.

"We want our farms! And we want you to go away, and never come back!" Martin said. "And if you do come back, we'll have some good old black tar on hand. Feathers really stick to that."

"Yeah!" Sam Pratt said. "If you ever come back here again, we'll kill you if we have to chase you clear to New York City, and even if you have half the United States army to back you up!"

"I—I won't come back!" Lanman's voice was almost a whisper. "But I—I didn't suppose—"

"You didn't suppose that men coming out here to carve a livelihood from the wilderness were smart enough to protect their homes, did you, Lanman?" Martin looked at him. "You didn't know that we happen to love this land we're on. We're putting down roots here. This is our land, and we'll defend it aganst the hounds of hell!"

"Why didn't you get a deed to it, then?"

"Some didn't have the money. Some were just too busy," the man named Bert said. "It was just something we put off until tomorrow."

"What about it, fellows? Shall we take him at his word?" Martin looked over the faces of the assembled settlers.

"Suits me," said Pratt, and all agreed.

They picked up Lanman's scattered garments, and handed them to him.

"Just a minute, fellows," Martin said. "I believe we'd better take the deed out of his coat tail pocket."

Lanman was too defeated to object, and Martin, reaching into the pocket pulled out the legal document on which was the signature of Martin Van Buren, President of the United States.

They threw snow on the fire, and began walking slowly back to the house. Only once did Lanman attempt to run away and Pamasaw quickly and deftly threw him to the ground.

Once inside the cabin Lanman, with a quavering hand deeded the thousand acres of land to the assembled pioneers in a group.

"But you aren't a company," said Lanman, "You all going to own it together?"

"That's no concern of yours," Martin answered, going over to a little box and taking out a clean sheet of paper.

Lanman started to go.

"Oh, don't be in such a hurry, Lanman. You're leaving without your money!" Martin smiled. "And then there's this little document I want you to sign. My wife will witness it."

"What document?" demanded Lanman.

"You'll see!" Martin wrote hurriedly on the paper, and handed it to Lanman. "Sign it, Lanman. Owaysa, you witness it."

Lanman took the quill pen in his hand, read it hurriedly, and signed the paper, then handed the pen to Owaysa.

"Now, we'll pay you," said Martin. "And with gold Spanish doubloons, silver dollars, and some British and French money for good measure. Lansman received his money, and went silently out the door without a backward glance."

As the sound of the sleighbells receded into the distance, the settlers gathered around Martin, and looked at the deed.

"But what's that other paper?" asked Sam.

Martin showed them the sheet of paper. It read:

> *White Panther Spring, Michigan, this 20th day of February, 1838.*
>
> *I, Berton Lanman, being of sound mind, and of my own free will and accord, do hereby certify that I will never again appear in Hillsdale County, Michigan on pain of being maple-sugared and feathered.*
>
> *Signed, Berton Lanman.*
>
> *Witnessed by Delia Langdon.*

18

In Which Matters Drift Towards Momentous Changes

Martin and his friends were unprepared for the greeting of their attorney, James Kinman, when they asked him to prepare the proper papers dividing the land among them.

"I believe you're the first men to beat a land shark like Lanman in what appears to be a legal way," Kinman smiled as he finished his work. "Now don't waste time filing the deeds. Get it straightened out at the county seat. Then I'm going to write it up in the Gazette.

"We don't want a lot of fanfare," Martin said. "We just want our farmlands."

"No, you don't want publicity, but maybe you've set up a method for dealing with these vultures." Kinman made no further statement, but the men lost no time in filing their deeds. They had had all they wanted of delay in this matter which had so nearly cost them their chosen holdings and the improvements such as some fencing, and crude buildings.

On arriving in Grannisville they went straightway to the log house of Salem T. King, the county registrar of deeds. King was a little man, wearing steel-rimmed spectacles up on his forehead which he now pulled down over his eyes to study the papers.

"Who's this John Jay?" he inquired, pushing the spectacles up on his forehead again, and looking around the room.

"I'm John Jay," and Pamasaw came forward.

"You?" King looked at him suspiciously. "What do you want of a snippet of land of only forty acres when your people claim the most of southern Michigan?"

"Your law is different from ours," Pamasaw answered. "All the people own *all* the land in *our* law. In yours, we own nothing. When the white man has bought up all the land where does the Indian go unless he owns some by *your* law?"

"But John Jay's not your name," King said. "I'm not going to register a deed to an Injun."

"Oh, yes you be!" the voice of one of the pioneers said. "Without him we wouldn't have had money enough."

King looked at the paper, turning it about curiously.

"Right legal document," he remarked. "I see Jim Kinman drew it up. Suppose if I don't register it he'll give me fits in the next issue of that newspaper of his."

When Pamasaw left the house of the registrar of deeds he clutched the document with a pride he had not known before. He was the first among all the tribe of Baw Beese to actually own in the eyes of all the world, a choice bit of real estate. That much of the land would be his to have and to hold even against the *Ke-moke-mon*, and he walked with majestic dignity down the tiny street with the pioneers.

But while Pamasaw, now to be known as John Jay, was sure of a place in a changing world, Kakatoma still languished in the Branch county jail.

The plight of Kakatoma was brought forcibly to the attention of Martin and Pamasaw, when, on entering the Great Sauk Inn Martin was handed a letter from Governor Mason.

"Just came today," said George Grannis, as he handed Martin the epistle. "You looking for some state office, Martin?"

Mystified, Martin tore open the letter, and read a strange request from the governor himself.

Martin Langdon, Esquire,
Grannisville, Michigan.
My Honored Friend, Langdon:

As you have previously proved yourself invaluable in giving accurate information to me concerning Indian affairs, I wish you to tell me exactly your opinion of an Indian called Kakatoma, accused of murdering an Indian Chief called Sau-en-quett on an island in a lake in Branch county.

He has, I understand, acted in accordance with Indian law contrary to the laws of the state. But as it is an

Indian matter I am wondering if the state would be wise in prosecuting this Indian.

Please look into this matter and advise me. I am beset by conflicting reports.

STEVENS T. MASON,
Governor of the
State of Michigan

"Bad news or good?" George Grannis could not restrain his curiosity.

Martin laid the letter on the counter before the tavern keeper and said, "Read it if you want to, George. I'm flattered by the governor's confidence in me."

George looked at Martin appraisingly after he had perused the letter. "You ought to run for the legislature," he said. "You'd get along with the governor, and maybe pound some sense into their heads down there at Detroit. Do you know they're actually moving the county seat to Hillsdale?"

"I've heard of it."

"But it's crooked! I've heard on good authority that E. B. Seelye has been offered six thousand dollars to get it through."

"Who said so, George?"

"Oh, I can't say. But we're organizing another company right here, and we're offering inducements. We want to put a town in the village where you were that time you broke your leg."

"What inducements?"

"Oh, free land for a tavern, and all that. And then we'll get the legislature to make that the county seat. It's nearer Seelye's home than Hillsdale. I think, however, if we play our cards right we can keep the county seat right here."

"Meshawa-od-dawn will be hard to pronounce, unless you give it the English equivalent, Elk Lake village. Or what were you going to call it?"

"We want an Indian name, Martin. But we want one they can pronounce. What was the name of the Indian that set your leg?"

"Osseo," Martin answered. "He's my father-in-law."

"Know what it means?"

"It means," said Pamasaw, entering the conversation for the first time, "son of the evening star."

"Good!" said George Grannis. "Now Martin, suppose you take along a surveyor some day and show him where this place is, and we'll honor you by naming it after your father-in-law. The governor's interested in Indian affairs, apparently, and that ought to please the Indians. None of them live there now, do they?"

"No, they moved away three or four years ago."

"Wait until I tell Morgan, and the rest of the men here. We'll beat Howder and Cook and Ferris at their own game. When can you go over to help survey it?"

Picking up his letter just received, Martin walked away from the counter as some emigrants came through the door to inquire the way to a place called Litchfield.

"Well now that would be where Bushnell took up some land," Grannis explained. "You leave here and go north on the Kalamazoo trail six or seven miles and you will come to the village, but as a word of advice, there's a mean Indian over there named Leathernose. They tell me he's pretty unpleasant at times and some of the settlers are afraid of him. Don't pick a fight with him—just feed him and the quas with him.

"To hell with the Injuns!" was the answer. "I've come out here to make my own livin'. Any Injun comes pesterin' me or the kids, he gets a musket ball between the eys."

"Well don't say I haven't warned you," George Grannis replied.

Without even so much as a 'thank you' for having been given directions to Litchfield, the party turned heel and went out the tavern door.

This episode brought very vividly to Martin's remembrance the series of events when Leathernose had been divested of what he had considered his holdings. Thoughtfully he stuffed his letter inside his leather jacket.

"See!" exclaimed Pamasaw. "Leathernose is a mean Indian—because Leathernose didn't own land by *Ke-moke-mon* law. But I own land now. Your law should keep that much for me."

"You mean to say you own land?" George Grannis asked Pamasaw.

Martin then offered the explanation that Pamasaw had bought forty acres along with the rest of them at the time they had made their purchase from the 'slicker' Lanman.

George, who was curious said, "No reason to ask, but how did you come out with him?"

Martin smiled and recounted the plot with relish.

"He's mighty lucky to get off with his life," George remarked. "I've known fellows like him to go out in the woods—I'm not saying where—to go out in the woods and never be heard of again. But you know they've always seemed to have sold their land. Somehow their names keep coming up on deeds. They just disappear."

"Land speculation is all right," Martin said. "But it should be *just* land. A fellow shouldn't sneak in and buy land that's been improved by squatters. That might be the answer as to why some of these land sharks are never heard of again."

"Well, when you going to help lay out this new village for us, Martin?" George Grannis was back on his favorite topic again—the county seat controversy.

"Believe I'd better look after the Governor's business first," Martin answered, and turning to Pamasaw he said, "We'd better go to Happy Waters together, Pamasaw."

The young Indian acquiesced in the matter, and they left the tavern. Martin sent word to Owaysa by Sam Pratt, who happened on the scene just then with supplies from Morgan's store.

*****

It was a simple matter to get permission from the sheriff of Branch county to talk to Kakatoma who showed little or no emotion as Martin and Pamasaw were led to his cell. With a note of amusement in his voice Martin said, "You don't seem so glad to see us."

Kakatoma's reaction was a baleful gleam in his eye.

"Why glad?" he spat out. "Pamasaw no friend. *You,* Ke-mokemon!"

Pamasaw's response to this statement was immediate and vituperous. Speaking in Potowatomi the two young men hurled Indian epithets at one another. Martin could only translate into English shch words as dog, skunk, snake, and horse thief. Only the barricade of the cell kept them from springing on one another.

The jailer commanded: "Speak English! You two! No more of yer damned Indian talk!"

"She got horse back!" Kakatoma shouted. "How I know you want 'em paleface qua?"

Pamasaw, momentarily embarrassed, appeared to ignore the affront and quickly demanded, "Do you or do you not want out of here?"

"Yes! Want to get out! Go to Chippewa, get big chiefs—"

"Idle bragging, Kakatoma," Martin replied. "You have nothing to be proud of. If you have so much influence with these 'big chiefs' you speak of, why hasn't even one of them come to your defense?"

"But Injun friends try. Me, I kill Sau-en-quett. Me hero! Council fires tell big tale—me like Hiawatha, or Manaboza!"

"Your name is not mentioned at our council fires," Pamasaw's statement was delivered in a flat and final tone.

"But Wenojah say in council fire my name big!"

"Wenojah thinks you're a big hero," Pamasaw retorted. "She wants to make you feel good."

Seeing this conversation was getting nowhere, Martin now demanded to know what Kakatoma would do once he was released.

For once, Kakatoma looked at Martin squarely in the eye. Then he looked at the burly deputy guarding the doorway and seeming to almost shrink inside himself finally admitted, "I—I don't know what I will do."

"Would you agree not to try to stir up your tribesmen into warfare?"

The Indian looked around the unfriendly, small cell. In his eyes as they turned on Martin, there was no look of defiance.

"If I get out," he said, "I hunt—I stay with wife."

"But you're not married," said Martin.

"Me get married to Wenojah!" Kakatoma could not resist a smile of triumph in Pamasaw's direction.

"Would she marry less than a hero?" Pamasaw asked.

"Me hero! Me kill Sau-en-quett! Law of knife!"

"I wouldn't be so proud of it," Martin said. "That's why you're here—for murder!"

"Here for planning Injun war!"

"You and yer Injun war!" the deputy sneered. "We ain't afeared none of no Injun war from the likes of you!"

Kakatoma, who had straightened up proudly when he spoke of himself as a hero, once more lost his air of bravado when reminded of his failure, and Martin now feeling himself to be somewhat sorry for him said, more gently, "You could only cause trouble—for your own people. And now, once more I ask you, what will you do if you are released or would you rather hang for murder?"

"I hunt! I get em wife!" Kakatoma said softly. "That all."

"Time's up!" said the deputy; and without further words Martin and Pamasaw left the cell, and after thanking the sheriff stepped outside the jail.

Wenojah was approaching with a basket on her arm. At first she lowered her eyes on seeing Pamasaw, and to all appearances had no intention of acknowledging their presence.

"Wenojah!" said Pamasaw.

"A-owh!" the girl answered and stopped.

The two conversed only in the Potowatomi tongue briefly, and the only thing Martin was able to understand was when she showed Pamasaw some cakes in the basket and indicated that she was taking them to Kakatoma.

The pair separated without apparent sentiment, and Martin did not find out what they had said to each other for many moons afterward.

19

Some Marriage Plans Go Awry

To mete out the farms in proportion to the amounts each settler had contributed would have been impossible for the pioneers. Their recorded deeds were replete with such statements as "containing 40 acres, more or less." The measurements as they had paced them off were only roughly accurate so long as they embraced the original thousand acres described in the deed issued to Lanman by the land office.

Every man had more land than he could work in 1839, but Martin knew the time would come that such descriptions as appeared on the deeds, and their own imaginary rough boundaries through the forest would prove troublesome.

He solved this very neatly by having George Grannis and his so-called Osseo Company provide the surveyors in return for his assistance.

All went peaceably throughout the spring, and with the maple syrup season starting late that year, it gave the pioneers longer than usual to participate in blazing boundary lines.

Pamasaw was the most curious of all the new land owners to view his small farm—on a portion of land his tribe still continued to claim as their own. The shore of the lake was swampy. But all lakes had swampy shores in this area. He looked at his choice of land with its many tall basswoods, hickories, birch, and ashes, with a few maples. Some of the pioneers had cleared their land whereas he would still have it all to do. But there was no hurry since he was in no immediate need of clearing more than just enough land for the erection of a bark house. He would try living alone in the forest, away from his people.

But Pamasaw was aware that his little acreage adjoined the farm of Anson Mergen, and consequently was not surprised while the snows were still on the ground, when Betsey appeared one sunny afternoon. He had just felled a birch tree, and was stripping it of its bark.

"Hello, John Jay!" she greeted him and giggled. "You see I know who my new neighbor is!"

Pamasaw paused in his work. Betsey was a strange contrast to the women at Ko-jess-sug-wa-seepe. Her red knitted mittens and dark cloth coat, her long skirt, and heavily-booted feet, gave her an appearance of solidity that belied his earlier observation of a very slender figure, back in the warmer days of summer. Her auburn hair peeped beneath a knitted cap, and the freckles on her face were almost gone. He wanted to say something, but found himself unable to think of what to say, except to casually remark, "It's very cold, hardly any maple syrup yet."

"Yes, it stays cold," Betsey agreed. "Why don't you build a fire so I can get warm?"

"Can't get warm outdoors unless you have a big fire," Pamasaw said. "Come back after I get the house done."

"Putting in a fireplace like the settlers?" she asked, sitting down on the birch log.

"I might. But I can't do stonework. It would have to be mud and sticks."

"That's like ours," Betsey said. "How did your people get along before the settlers came and showed you how to do things?"

"They got along very well." Pamasaw felt like saying that he believed they got along better, but thought it an unwise remark.

"When spring comes, I'm going to have to marry Elihu Chapin," she announced in a matter of fact tone. Pamasaw interpreted it as sounding bleak. At least he hoped it was.

"You've told me so before," he said, and began self-consciously to fit a piece of bark to the side of his house. "Your mother has told me about it, and your father has almost warned me."

Betsey giggled. "What do you mean, warned?"

He hesitated. "Seemed to be afraid that I—well I don't know—afraid I might say something ..." his voice drifted off but Betsey persisted.

"And what might you say, Pamasaw?" Her eyes twinkled mischievously.

He concentrated on the large piece of bark, pretending to be very busy. Finally he replied, "Oh I don't know, just things I guess—maybe something I'd be sorry for." He dared not look into her eyes. She might read his mind. Even if he could tell her what good would it do?

One thing was certain, his feelings were far different than those he had had for Wenojah whom he had intended to marry because of his manitou. But this was different. Many thoughts rushed through his mind. How does one describe flying birds, the wayward winds, the mists of dawn, the sweet flavor of honey, the eyes of a fawn, the rainbow in the sky...?

"There's no one around to hear you Pamasaw," Betsey arose from the log and stepped close to him. He dropped the piece of bark onto the snow and looked out across the frozen lake.

"I—I don't know." And then he turned and looked her squarely in the eyes.

"Tell me Pamasaw," she said softly, "is it something so bad as all that?"

Still no words came. Instead he found himself suddenly drawing her close in his arms, and for one wild, mad moment he found himself transported to a world the other side of the moon.

Suddenly she turned away. There were tears in her eyes. "I'm a bad woman," she thought and confronting Pamasaw again she said, "I had no right to come here! I made my promise to marry Elihu. He's a lot older than you, Pamasaw, but lonely. You see his first wife died, and there are no children. Pa is set on the marriage, because...well because he says that Elihu is rich and will make me a good husband even though he is a little odd. Besides, coming out here—well most of the settlers have wives already, either here or back east where they've come from. Oh, I don't want to marry him, Pamasaw... but neither does Pa want an old maid on his hands!"

Pamasaw sighed as he stooped over to pick up a piece of bark which had fallen from his hands but suddenly they felt cold and fumbling as he tried to replace it against the framework.

"So he is rich. I should have known." There was deep sorrow in Pamasaw's voice. Shuniah, always shuniah that the Long Knives want...I'm just an Indian, and a poor one at that." A faint gleam of sunlight shone for a moment through the trees, and he sighed. Love was like that...a faint touch and no longer there. He didn't dare to tell her...how fragile, how delicate, how very precious was this feeling in his heart for her. He must speak to his manitou about it.

As though she discerned what was going on in his mind she said to him, "You are very shy, Pamasaw. Are all Indian braves like that? We've always heard terrible tales back east of Indians scalping women, and... and even worse things that that."

"Like what?" he asked.

"Well, well you know...like taking advantage of them and awful things like that."

Pamasaw smiled in spite of the sadness in his heart. Her mystery and charm were so apparent. "I will tell you," he answered. "Indian braves are...yes, they are very shy with a woman they love." Resuming work on his bark house he didn't turn to watch Betsey as she hurried away.

Try as he would he could not forget that fraction of a minute that had seemed like an eternity of bliss. Betsey should never marry Elihu, he thought, as he continued his work.

But neither, if he was true to his manitou, had he a right to think of marriage. But one thought consoled him. Betsey had certainly been born many miles away from his village. But Anson Mergen had not been a great chief. The *Ke-moke-mon* did not have chiefs.

Then he suddenly thought that possibly Anson had held a high office in his former home. If he had, that would be possibly what his manitou was trying to tell him.

He made up his mind he would settle that point. There could be no harm in finding out, so he went to Martin and asked him if he knew.

Martin reflected a moment before answering. "Well Pamasaw, I've been somewhat curious too, but I really don't know. I've never asked him and he's never offered any information. But I've noticed that he never seems to lack money or the essentials. I've just had the idea that he came out here as a settler to add more to what he already has like so many others. But I think I know what you have in mind," he continued, pausing to throw some hay in front of the cow in the stanchion, "but it's too late now. Elihu's coming to marry Betsey next week. The date has been set which is Friday, the twenty-second of March."

Pamasaw acted embarrassed. He walked to the barn door, and

then said awkwardly, "How do you know what I'm thinking, Martin?"

"I'm not blind, and neither is anybody else. Elihu's a widower, needs another wife, and Betsey's his promised bride. She's taken a fancy to you and you to her, but it's too late."

"Not until she s married," Pamasaw said stubbornly. "She doesn't love him."

"Well Anson Mergen is all for it and says he's a fine man, even if he is a little old."

"People shouldn't marry unless they care for each other," Pamasaw insisted.

"Now see here, Pamasaw. How could you look after Betsey if you had her?"

"I have forty acres," he smiled. "Isn't that enough?"

"No, it's not enough. You don't have the know-how. And furthermore, the Mergens have laid great store on Betsey's marriage to Elihu who is undoubtedly an old friend of theirs and deserving of a good wife like Betsey. Arrangements are all made and we're all invited to the wedding. You can't stop preparations like that. It's going to be a big affair."

"But just the same, I want to know what Ansom Mergen did before he came here. That can't hurt anybody, can it?"

"It won't do any good, but I'll try and find out," Martin started for his cabin and then stopped. Feeling compassion in his heart for Pamasaw and his troubled love affairs he said, "Come along and have supper with Owaysa and me." Ordinarily nothing would have pleased him more, but tonight he must refuse. He must be alone. He must confer with his manitou. There must be an answer.

Wenojah was no longer of any consequence. He had somehow misinterpreted his vision. It simply wasn't possible that he could have been in love with her all that time. He remembered the little melody he had composed just for her, and wondered how he could have imagined being in love with one so unreasonable and cold—one who had insisted on the absurdity of driving out all the *Ke-moke-mon* before considering marriage. So far as he was concerned now, he wouldn't give an old broken arrow for such a foolish girl. Driving out the pioneers was about as absurd an idea as one could imagine. It would be like attempting to prevent the sun from rising in the morning. More and more in increasing numbers the settlers were pouring in.

Pamasaw was not aware that a personal invitation was necessary to attend the wedding. Indians enjoyed festivities, and liked being included in them as well as in barn raisings, house raisings and other activities, and Martin had said, "All are invited." He felt a little self-conscious because if Martin knew of his feeling for Betsy wouldn't everybody else know about it too. What he was really feeling was the humiliation of a jilted lover. He looked down at his hands. His skin was dark but actually no darker than some of the pioneers. He looked about his bark house. He had left a hole in the roof for the smoke from the fire to escape. Betsey would have wanted a fireplace. This, he had omitted for the time being.

One thing perplexed him, however. Why did he not feel hopeless in the matter? Martin had said it was too late, but he refused to believe it.

*****

From the edge of a clearing near Mergen's cabin Pamasaw watched the arrival of some of the wedding guests. The minister, he recognized as the Rev. Darius Barker who had held the service in Howder's tavern.

All appeared in their fine clothes—clothes such as Pamasaw had never worn. Even Owaysa, who came later than the others was wearing a full blue skirt like the settler's wives.

And now his thoughts returned to the melody he wanted to play for Betsey. He wanted the tune to tell his yearnings, his sorrows, his devotion. It must be a voice that spoke of utter dreariness of being left alone and yet another note crept in, a little note like sunshine that lightened up the gloom. He shook his head in puzzlement.

After a while he fingered the flute inside his jacket. If Betsey would only appear now he would improvise this melody for her. The sound of the flute would reach the clearing where some of the pioneers were standing smoking their pipes. If only Betsey would appear, but the women all remained discreetly indoors.

Time passed slowly as he waited. It was early spring, and a steady drizzle was starting to make his vantage point uncomfortable. Finally, without further inner qualms in the matter, he walked boldly out into the open and straight to the front door of the cabin.

"You here, Pamasaw?" Martin asked in surprise, as he reached the cabin door. The others had gone inside, and Martin was the last to leave the open air, knocking the ashes from his pipe against the log wall.

"I'm here!" Pamasaw said. "I've come to the wedding!" With no further explanation he stepped inside. Some sprigs of evergreen had been festooned along the walls, but the tiny room was so crowded there was scarcely space to stand. There was utter silence in the room which had been sounding like a flock of chattering blackbirds.

"Pamasaw!" Betsey was unaware her hoarse whisper carried throughout the room.

Mergen started to shoulder his way towards Pamasaw. But Mrs. Mergen, who evidently was frightened, restrained him.

Pamasaw, his heart doing strange things within his breast, pulled out his flute.

"I have a tune for your wedding day, Betsey," he said. His voice sounded strange and unnatural.

All eyes were upon him as he placed the mouthpiece of his flute to his lips. He began to play—a plaintive, weird strain, sounding like the lament of a dying soul. Betsey's eyes filled with tears she could no longer restrain. Pamasaw lost the sequence of his improvised melody and was compelled to stop.

Mergen burst from the restraining hand of his wife.

"Get out of here with that thing!" he yelled. "You've made my little girl cry!"

Pamasaw, humiliated because he had forgotten the tune, was glad to leave. But he knew now what he had wanted to find out. Betsey was unhappy about the wedding. He fled speedily to the confines of his own bark house.

He sat down on his fragrant bed of cedar boughs covered with a blanket. Again fingering the notes on his flute he found he could play the melody now. Over and over he played it. After a while he built a fire and the interior of his bark house was bright and warm. But his heart remained sad and contemplative.

BETSEY, when she saw Pamasaw standing there playing his flute in her cabin on her wedding day, immediately sensed that the melody so hauntingly sad—before he stopped so abruptly—expressed not only his, but her own feelings. She tried to smile at the guests but her eyes would fill with tears.

"Come Betsey, you've got to get hold of yourself," her mother said impatiently, "it's bad luck to cry at your wedding."

"You don't understand, Ma," she said softly, drying her eyes again, aware that the wedding guests were watching her curiously.

"Damned Injuns!" exploded Anson. "Nobody asked him to the wedding! Imagine busting in like that and saying he had a tune for her wedding day. He must be crazy!"

The other guests mostly agreed it was strange, indeed. Now they were growing restive. The bridegroom had not appeared and even the Rev. Mr. Barker found the hour was getting late.

"I'm sorry, Mr. Mergen," he said. "But I have a special meeting with the vestry tonight, and I must be going in order to get to Grannisville before dark."

As one by one the wedding guests found that it was getting chore time, they too were growing restive and uneasy.

"Can't imagine what could have happened to Elihu," Anson said. "I've laid great store by this wedding. But he'll be along, I'm sure."

However, regardless of Anson's desire for more time in the matter the guests all departed, leaving only Martin and Owaysa.

Betsey felt rather glad that there had been that interruption from Pamasaw, for when the tears were about to roll down her cheeks she knew it would not be an easy matter to be the darling young wife of an old widower she did not love. When she had made the promise before coming west with her parents she had not yet met Pamasaw. Well, at least she would be living some twenty miles further away from him and his cabin and if she never saw him again just knowing that he loved her would make it easier to endure a bleak marriage in order to please her father.

Had it not been for that moment beside the birch log a few weeks ago she could have endured the wedding a great deal better. But that moment had been her undoing. It was strange. She had been instantly drawn to him from the very beginning. He was handsome and manly and he spoke such good English. His skin was not very dark, no really much darker than many sun-tanned pioneers. He was darker than Owaysa, it was true. But what difference did it really make? Wasn't love, after all, more important than pleasing ones' parents?

Betsey's mother, however, was not one in whom she could confide her heart's desires. But she knew that her mother laid no such store on Elihu Chapin as did her father who had also said, "He'll die before you, and then you'll be free and a rich widow. Almost every man admires a rich widow."

"How awful to talk that way! To put such ideas into Betsey's head! Shame on you!" her mother had stormed.

But now it was today. The day of her wedding, and she knew in her heart what she felt a few weeks ago. It was Pamasaw she wanted. His name on the deed was John Jay. She would rather be Mrs. John Jay than Mrs. Elihu Chapin. But there seemed no way out. How could she just up and leave with all the wedding guests there and the wedding presents on the table?

But now the guests had left, and the minister was gone. She felt a sudden elation. Perhaps Elihu was dead. Maybe a bear might have eaten him. What a wicked thought. She must ask God to forgive her.

She was about to change her dress to something simpler when Anson shouted from outside.

"Here he comes, now!"

Betsey and her mother went to the front door of the cabin, and there, coming into the yard was the strangest vehicle ever beheld. It was an ox card with only one ox, and in the yoke at the other side was Elihu himself. One wheel of the cart was broken, and the axle was dragging on the ground.

"Had some pesky bad luck," said Elihu, getting out of his ox yoke. Had an ex brake, and then one of the oxen up and got mired down. But I 'lowed nothin' was goin' to interfere with my weddin'! So here I be!"

"You, Elihu! You ought to be ashamed of yourself!" said Anson. "With all the money you've got coming in clothes like that, and in an ox cart!"

"Clothes was all right at first. Just got ripped up a mite," Elihu said. "And I figger if an ox cart's good enough fer me, it's good enough fer my wife."

Betsey shook her auburn curls, and screamed, "I'll never marry an ox!"

She dashed into the cabin, swooped her wedding presents into an apron, dashed out the back door and headed straight for Pamasaw's bark house, before her parents even knew she had left. She could still hear them arguing with Elihu as she tramped through the wet leaves of the forest. She looked down at her muddy shoes. "Never, and I mean NEVER do I want to see that man again!" Betsey was unaware that she had spoken those words out loud. She was answered by a sudden "Whooo!" For a moment she thought she'd drop dead. It was only a startled owl and she quickly recovered her balance. And now through the fast-falling dusk came the sad-sweet lament once more. Smoke was curling from the hole in the roof. She quickly entered the cabin.

"Pamasaw!" she cried, "I couldn't go through with it!" She flung the apron containing the wedding presents down beside him. As though he could hardly believe his eyes, he laid aside his flute and with all the dignity of a fine gentleman brought up in one of the finest schools in the east, he took her in his arms.

"We must hurry," she urged, "before they find us!"

"Where will we go?"

"To find a minister, of course! We've got to run away... to elope ... before my father finds us."

Pamasaw could hardly believe his good fortune, as she hurriedly narrated the events of the afternoon, and after she had finished asked, "But where can we find a minister who will marry us?"

"In Grannisville, of course," she answered. "But Pamasaw we must hurry!"

But instead of going straight to Grannisville, Pamasaw led Betsey to the cabin of Martin and Owaysa to borrow another horse.

Martin said he would gladly loan them the horse, but as the Rev. Darius Barker was inside perhaps he could perform the ceremony right there.

Betsey's explanation of what happened to Elihu and his strange accoutrements for his wedding set them in a hilarious mood.

"You are indeed fortunate," said the Rev. Mr. Barker. Had I not had to stop to repair a bridle on my own horse, I should have been gone long before now."

And so it was, in the cabin of Martin and Owaysa, that Betsey Mergen became the bride of Pamasaw. But on the register, Mrs. John Jay.*

*NOTE: This episode from pioneer life is told in the poem "Eliphalet Chapin's Wedding" in Will Carleton's book *Farm Festivals.*

20

Sadness Befalls Squawfield

Had it not been for spring work the marriage of Pamasaw, known officially as John Jay and Betsey Mergen might have been a topic of conversation longer than it was.

But after Anson Mergen had sputtered about his daughter marrying "an Indian savage," and Elihu Chapin had expressed his anger at the outrage, and returned on foot to his own holdings east of Adrian, matters subsided in the neighborhood to the customary routine of frontier life—wood cutting, chores, plowing and planting.

Pamasaw constructed a chimney at one end of his bark house after the manner of the settlers, and was prevailed on to add a couple of windows and a wooden door. His carpenter work was crude indeed, but he could fashion wooden spoons and plates with surprising skill.

The Mergens, although at first saying they never could forgive their daughter for marrying an Indian soon found themselves so lonely that they softened in their attitude. It was hard, however, to accept Pamasaw as a son-in-law. At one time they had wanted to have the marriage annulled, but no such proceedings were known in the courts in Hillsdale county in 1839.

Finally, at Anson's request, Mrs. Mergen had called on Betsey in her primitive bark house, with only two windows.

Betsey welcomed her mother with the tenderness of a loving daughter. Her mother looked around the bark house with a somewhat disapproving eye. She sat on an upended chunk of wood being used for a chair.

"Not much like what you're used to, is it, Betsey?"

"It's better than living with old Elihu!"

"Maybe your marriage will work out, Betsey. But how many other wives has he got?"

"Why none, Ma! How you talk. Pamasaw thinks he was guided by what he calls his manitou to marry me. Actually I was the one that guided him."

"Betsey! You shock me. After all, you're the daughter of a former member of the legislature. And if the Whigs had stayed in power we might still have been back east."

"And that's just why he thinks his manitou guided him to marry me. His manitou, he says, informed him he was to marry the daughter of a great chief born a distance from his village."

"Huh!" Mrs. Mergen sniffed. "Well, I do declare! Believes in witchcraft too, I suppose! And do you think Anson's a great chief?"

"Well, Ma, you know that Pa was a lot more important than just an ordinary farmer back east."

"Have you ever wondered how this fellow's going to support you?"

"Why, if the worst comes to the worst we could go and live in the village at Squawfield."

"Great snakes, Betsey! Don't be telling me my daughter's got to live in an Indian village!"

"Well, that's only if the worst comes to the worst. But Pamasaw knows a lot about getting things to eat in the forest. He's a good hunter and a good fisherman—"

"Now Betsey, hunting and fishing are all right, but farming is what makes the mare go in this country. Yes siree! You've got to have something more than hunting and fishing if you're going to make enough to keep body and soul together. Now if you'd come home and help me, we can get that Indian of yours started doing something useful."

"I resent having you call him 'that Indian'. He's in love with me, and he isn't just an Indian. He's my husband."

"That's well and good, but he might as well learn to be a farmer. Besides, Betsey," Mrs. Mergen's tone softened, "we're powerful lonesome. And if you'll come back, we—we'll give you and your—well —your husband, half of everything we make."

The proposition sounded excellent to Betsey and when her mother had left and Pamasaw had returned from a hunting expedition with only a rabbit, she talked the matter over with him.

Pamasaw agreed that the offer was tempting, but he would not move into the same house with Betsey's parents.

"But we're going to have to get through next winter somehow, Pamasaw."

"I know. I don't make enough shuniah!"

"Pa can teach you a lot about farming," Betsey put a kettle on the crane in the fireplace.

"Listen, Betsey, I've too much pride to lean on your pa. But if he wants to teach me how to farm, and let us live here by ourselves, I'll give it a try."

So it was arranged that Pamasaw would work with Anson Mergen who did not object too strenuously to letting the young people live alone together. The lumber for the new farm house was cut and in the farmyard, but the erection of it would have to wait until after harvest.

Throughout the summer months Pamasaw learned to handle a scythe to cut marsh grass, and a cradle for harvesting wheat. He even mastered the art of milking a cow; and of mixing the swill to feed the squealing hogs.

Sometimes, when the crows were cawing raucously, or the bob-whites whistled urgently, he wished he could forget these irksome labors and wander in the woods, or by a shady stream where trout were running. But this was his education in how to make *shuniah,* just as he had laboriously learned to speak what was to him originally the foreign language of the settlers. For despite the fact that English had been spoken in the area for nearly a hundred years, few Indians could understand it and fewer still could converse in it fluently.

And then one day the event that changed the destinies of the people in southern Michigan forever, occurred. It seemed trivial at the time, and few realized the significance of the fact that some boys swimming in a lake could have such far-reaching consequences.

A white boy in his teens named Warren Champlin, whose parents lived near Squawfield, went swimming with some Indian boys in a nearby lake. It was a hot day in late July. Warren left his little brother on the shore, with some smaller Indian boys, while he and the older youths got into a canoe and paddled out to swim in deep water. Suddenly the terrified screams of Warren's young brother shattered the primeval stillness of the forest along the lake shore.

As well as the swimmers in the lake who heard the screams, there was also Ed Maxon, at work in a nearby field. He arrived in time to see some Indian boys brandishing a knife around the scalp lock of the little boy.

Warren and the older boys tried to console the terrified child, while the Indian boys said they had been teasing him by telling him they were going to scalp him.

Maxon, striding forward, addressed Warren triumphantly: "You see don't ye, they purty nigh got yer little brother!"

"It was all in fun! He'll recover," Warren replied.

"Fun, nothin'! You was swimmin'! If I hadn't come just when I did he'd o' been scalped! That's what!"

From that minute on the voice of Ed Maxon was heard in Ame's store in Keene. It was heard in Morgan's store in Grannisville and in Howder's tavern in Hillsdale.

"The Injuns is troublesome!" Maxon repeated over and over. "And by the great salt mackerel they're goin' west, or I'm sendin' every damned redskin to the happy hunting ground myself."

Maxon wrote President VanBuren. He wrote senators and he wrote congressmen. It did not matter that his scrawl was illiterate. What mattered was that it sounded urgent.

The countryside was agog, and the tales in repetition grew out of proportion to the truth.*

Pamasaw was incensed when Betsey came from her mother's with the story that "Little Charley Champlin was nearly scalped by the Indians, and only saved by the interference of Ed Maxon."

Pamasaw sought his old friend, Martin, to whom he felt he could always turn for assistance.

"Everybody knows," said Pamasaw, "that Maxon wants that land! Can't you do something to stop this talk, Martin?"

"I suppose we're the last ones to hear this tale," Martin stated, "but I can write Governor Mason the truth."

But Governor Mason's reply to Martin's letter was negative. It was in late August when the answer came from the Governor's office in Detroit. Owaysa, whose pregnant condition had been quite normal was feeling ill and nauseated and Martin hated to disclose the contents of the letter he received that day at Grannisville. He wadded it up and threw it on the embers in the fireplace.

"What did the Governor say?" she asked.

* NOTE: This episode is recounted in Hogaboam's *History of the Bean Creek Country.*

"Says it's too late for him to do anything about it!" Martin slumped dejectedly onto a chair.

"Not do anything? The Governor of the state of Michigan?"

"He says the matter is out of his hands. A Brevet Major named Brady at Fort Gratiot has been delegated to get the Indians out of here. President VanBuren signed the order. He receives three dollars a head for every brave, squaw and papoose that he takes to Iowa."

"But Martin!" Owaysa's voice was fraught with emotion. "They haven't the right! Baw Beese never signed a treaty."

"Governor Mason says the Treaty of Chicago in 1833 gives them the right. Topinabee signed. So did Moquago."

Owaysa was silent, and they both sat downhearted and sad watching the dull glow of embers smoldering in the ashes.

"Does the Governor say when?" Owaysa finally asked.

"Just 'soon'! Maxon's been working on it for over a year."

"Will they take them all, Martin?"

"All? I assume they will, Owaysa."

"Even my father?"

"I don't know."

"And what about Pamasaw — what of me?"

"Pamasaw they might take. But remember that John Jay has a title to land. If he stays in blue jeans and insists he's John Jay they can't touch him."

"And me?"

"You're my wife. I'd fight the whole army before I'd let them take you."

"I find it hard to believe this is happening," Owaysa said. "It's as though the earth was being suddenly made into the moon."

They sat in silence for a few minutes, before Martin continued: "Governor Mason is freeing Kakatoma. He said after going over the matter carefully from my report he is ordering the Branch county prosecutor to *nolle prosequi* the case."

*****

KAKATOMA was no longer wearing his fine buckskin clothes, but was garbed in an old blue shirt and blue jeans. Wenojah had taken his fine things home with her. The sheriff, however, had retained possession of his tomahawk and knife.

Kakatoma's skin was lighter than it had ever been due to his long confinement, and he felt weaker than he had ever felt before. Only a few of his friends had been to see him. The food during his stay in jail was not very good. There was a large quantity of salt pork which he detested. Had it not been for the ministrations of Wenojah, the Meadowlark, he might have gone quite hungry; for she came often to visit him always bringing some good Indian beans, or cakes.

But Kakatoma was astonished the day all this came to an end. For nearly a year he had been confined in a stinking cell.

Suddenly the door had been unlocked and opened and the deputy sheriff stood there with his keys in his hand.

"Come on! Get the hell out of here! And go as far away as you can. The Boy Wonder we've got for Governor says to *nolle pros* your case!"*

Kakatoma was suspicious that it was a trick. "What's *nolle pros?*" he asked.

"Fergit it! That's what it means! Come on, git out of here and see you don't git in no more trouble!"

They handed him his tomahawk and knife, and Kakatoma walked out into the open air. The sun was so bright it hurt his eyes for a few minutes. The air smelled good! It was the air of late summer before a rain. Everything had a dry green appearance.

When his eyes became used to his surroundings he could see that many changes had ensued since Sau-en-quett had deeded Mick-e-sawbe to the Long Knives. It had, in that brief span become the town of Coldwater. There was not a trace of the former Indian village left.

"Coldwater!" he said, thinking in his native Potawatomi. "Why must the Long Knives change its name from Happy Waters?" The water was not especially cold; but so far as that went, how could the waters be happy any more with all these pale foreigners surrounding them?

He looked down at his ragged jeans and his torn old shirt. He hoped Wenojah had carefully kept his leather leggins and jacket as she had said. He tucked his tomahawk into his belt, along with his knife and began walking in the general direction of Nottawa Seepe, and Wenojah.

*NOTE: Governor Mason actually did so order in this case of Kakatoma.

He was weak from his long confinement and he soon found himself instead of walking in the graceful gliding gait of the Indian, shuffling along like an old man. More than once he stopped to rest and once he even became so thirsty he stopped at a cabin of one of the *Ke-moke-mon* and asked for a drink of water.

The man seemed friendly enough, and not only gave him the water, but invited him inside for something to eat.

"Wife's gone to Coldwater for supplies," the man said. "But I've got a little jerked bear meat if you want it."

Kakatoma ate the bear meat. It was too salty, but it was a variation to his diet at the jail.

"Want a job?" asked the man.

"Job?" Kakatoma hardly knew the meaning of the word.

"I need a hired man. Can't pay much, but you look peeked, as though you'd been out of work a long time."

Kakatoma did not want to do paleface work. He only wanted to get to the Indian village where he could rest and smell the fragrance of the forest, and eat again some good Indian food.

"Have job," he finally answered. "Over by Dry Prairie."

"Oh!"

Kakatoma offered to split some wood for his meal, but the pioneer said he had plenty of wood, "Too damn much wood!" he explained.

When he resumed his journey Kakatoma felt refreshed, but darkness enshrouded the world before he could reach his destination. As he laid down on the bare ground in the forest he was aware that the earth smelled good. He was free! The thought kept repeating itself over and over in his mind. Never again would he wish to be anything but free! Above all else a man needed freedom—freedom to breathe fresh air, to sleep on the ground, outdoors! This indeed was far better than confinement, even in a nice cabin such as Martin and Owaysa had.

When, at last he reached the clearing near the village of Nottawa Seepe, the next forenoon, he was even more weary than ever. His wasted leg muscles would no longer support him. He lay down on the ground and slept. Nobody had come to welcome him. Nobody knew that he was there and that he was free.

21

The End Of An Era

To Martin and Owaysa the news that United States soldiers were to forcibly take the Indians west came as a shock. To most of the other pioneers and even the Mergens, it came as a disappointment, for most of them had staunch friends among the Indians, but to the Indians the news was a tragedy.

"Sioux kill me—kill us all!" Chief Baw Beese wailed dolefully, when he arrived at Martin's cabin with Owaysa's father, Osseo.

"Mebbe not kill all!" Osseo said. "Mebbe we go to good hunting ground. I go see."

"You mustn' go, Father. The Sioux are our mortal enemies. Can't you send one of the young men, Baw Beese?"

"Ugh!" the chief grunted. "Young men have hot blood! They get mad easy—get in trouble. Old man, like Osseo, wise."

With little delay Osseo, much against the wishes of Owaysa, set out on horseback to view the distant land in Iowa. He was to report back to the Indians at Ko-jess-sug-wa-seepe.

Martin was dubious about the trip. "He may not have time to get there and back. Nobody knows exactly when Brady and his soldiers will put in an appearance."

"He will never be back." Owaysa's eyes moistened with tears. "The Sioux will kill him. No Potowatomi ever travelled into that country and came back alive. The only word of their language my father knows is, *"How! How!* for our word, *Posho!"*

But as the weeks passed without further word of any expedition from Fort Gratiot, a woeful spectacle of Indian families going northward along the Kalamazoo trail began.

It was a pitiful sight to Martin as he watched them making their way northward with a horse on which a brave rode, and to which was attached a drag carrying his few possessions, followed by his wife, usually with a *kanogan* on her back with a baby facing backward in Indian style. Occasionally they would wave good-bye, but generally they marched stoically along looking neither to the right nor left.

"Where are these people going?" Martin asked Baw Beese one day when no less than three such caravans passed by his cabin.

"Go to land of Chippewa!" the chief answered. "Say they not wait for Osseo. Land west of Mississippi no good. Chippewa part of Three Council Fires. They friends—so stay in Michigan, not go west."

"It's shameful!" Owaysa burst out. "Our people have been good to the pioneers—there's never been any trouble."

Pamasaw on his way home from getting some supplies in Grannisville, stopped at the cabin, and seeing his father stated, "I've met three of our men on the trail today, who say they're going north of Jacksonburg to join the Chippewa."

The chief smiled. "They think that best way out. You not go there. No, you go west with tribe when time come!"

Pamasaw looked at his father in astonishment. "With Betsey?" he asked.

"You son of Baw Beese. You go with Betsey or not. But you go!"

"No!" Pamasaw, for the first time in his entire life had spoken sharply to his father. "I've always lived here. I own land. I stay here!"

"You own all outdoors! *Ke-moke-mon* not own! He take!"

"But I have a deed to my land from the United States, father. It is mine and mine alone. My name is John Jay. My farm will always be a place where Indians can come and visit."

"No!" Baw Beese's voice was rising angrily. "You little farm not like Injun land! You Injun, not *Ke-moke-mon!* You come when we go, or you no longer son of Baw Beese! I find new son in Ko-jess-sug-wa-seepe!"

"But Betsey's expecting a child, the same as Owaysa! She can't go west with me!"

"Then let stay!"

"No!" Pamasaw looked defiantly at his father. Baw Beese, regal in his native buckskins was the commanding chieftain, making a strange contrast to his son in blue jeans, but Pamasaw's defiance could have been no more pronounced had he been wearing war paint.

"Does paleface woman mean more than me—your father—your mother—your people?" the chief asked in Potowatomi.

Pamasaw, answering in his native tongue, attempted to placate his father. "My wife is with child, father. My child means a great deal to me. I have witnessed the encroachment of the Long Knives, and either we must change, or they must. They will not change, so we must. I respect your wisdom in Indian and tribal matters. I shall ever be ready to welcome you into my home as in times past, but I choose to remain here on land that I have bought from the Long Knives. When I married Betsey I knew that it meant forsaking the old ways, and it has not been easy for me. But should I leave Betsey now it would be like leaving half of my heart behind. I shall not leave her."

"Then I shall name another young man as my son. I shall call him Baw Bee," the chief continued speaking in his native tongue. "And when the time comes that the soldiers take us away, you will see me, your father, for the last time. I shall never return."

Pamasaw felt some qualms as he watched his father ride off towards his village. His father's attitude would never change—never soften. But Pamasaw had made his choice. He was casting his lot forever with the *Ke-moke-mon.* But the Indian blood in him welled up, and he too could act the stolid, apparently emotionless man so many settlers believed the Indian to be. He was quite capable of assuming an aloof exterior, pretending never to be hurt.

When news of the intended move of the United States government reached Moquago at Nottawa Seepe, he shrugged and made the simple statement, "I shall not go."

Kakatoma, however, was of a different opinion. "Perhaps the Sioux will not kill us," he said. "Perhaps they'll be our friends, and we can join forces with them and prevent the Long Knives from encroaching on our new lands across the Mississippi."

"It would be better to be free among the Sioux," Wenojah stated, "than to be prisoners here, surrounded by palefaces."

*****

WHEN the detachment of soldiers arrived at Keene, Maxon was there to meet them by a pre-arranged plan, and awaited their arrival at the Ames trading post.

When Major Brady put in his appearance and inquired for Maxon, he was taken aback when the intrepid veteran of the War of 1812 presented himself, managing a salute remembered from his army days.

"Here I be, Major, ready to take ye to Squawfield."

"How far is it?" Major Brady asked.

"As the crow flies, I'd say five or six miles," Maxon answered. "But better not move in on 'em until after dark. Some stragglers might be out until then. Of course, Major, I don't like to tell ye your business, you bein' a military man and all, but them Injuns is all-fired afeared of bayonets. Just surround their village, and close in with bayonets and you've got 'em!"

Major Brady could have informed Maxon he was well aware of such tactics but refrained from doing so. Pretending to take Maxon's advice, the detachment loitered about the trading post until twilight, and then went along the trail that led to Squawfield.

Moving with caution and under the cover of darkness, they surrounded the village, and standing poised with fixed bayonets, awaited the order to close in when the first red streaks of dawn appeared.

Major Brady gave the order to the trumpeter, and then Maxon impatiently shouted: "Come on and get up, ye lazy, good-fer-nothin' redskins!"

In an instant the barking of dogs, the screaming of terrified children, and the shouts and wails of both women and half-naked braves, echoed through the forests in the scarlet dawn of October 31, 1839.

The women and children sought the refuge of the friendly woods, but the ever diminishing circle of glistening bayonets drove them back like sheep at bay to the narrow confines of a few bark huts.

"Get your horses and your belongings!" Major Brady ordered. "You're going to a better place for Indians!"

Chief Baw Beese and Ash-te-wette came dejectedly from their lodge. Old Goon-pa-shee appeared and pronounced an Indian curse on the soldiers, the *Ke-moke-mon* and on the United States government. But the Indians observed that nothing immediately happened. No thunderbirds spread their wings in the orange light of the dawn. No water panthers rose out of the creek to attack the blue-coated

Long Knives. The threatening ring of bayonets, now close together remained immobile.

At last, after much weeping on the part of the women, all was in readiness for the sad journey they were about to undertake. When the last of the stragglers had been herded together, Maxon was gleeful. With the assistance of some of the soldiers, he put the torch to the flimsy bark dwellings, which burned like tinder, the flames shooting skyward quickly, leaving only blackened ruins of what had once been the homes of a couple of hundred people

But Maxon was not satisfied with only leaving Squawfield completely destroyed. His hatred knew no bounds, and no sooner had he been satisfied that not a vestige of Indian culture remained on what he called "my land," than he rushed forward and overtook Major Brady.

"Some of the red devils don't live here!" he said. "Some have already left. But there's an Injun girl livin' with a feller named Langdon, and a young Injun what up and run off with a settler's daughter. Snatched her right away from her intended husband, he did!"

"Where are they?" demanded the major.

"I'll show ye!" Maxon promised. "They're all further up the trail."

But when the sad cortege, chanting a melancholy melody reached the cabin of Anson Mergen and the major had knocked on the door, he was informed by Mergen himself, that Maxon must be in error.

"My daughter's not married to an Indian," Mergen said. "There's a mistake somewhere. She married a man named John Jay."

"He's lyin' ! John Jay's an Injun!" shouted Maxon.

"John Jay is a property owner," Mergen said stoutly.

"Where is he?" demanded Major Brady.

"I don't believe, Major, the whereabouts of my son-in-law is any of your particular business," Mergen answered. "My home is my castle, and you may not enter it!"

The major accepted the rebuff with poor grace, and apologized if he had been insolent, and turning to Maxon said, "I believe Maxon, that we will be in trouble if we press this matter further."

Maxon sputtered that, "all damned redskins should go, no matter who or what they were."

"I only get three dollars a head for them, delivered across the Mississippi," said Major Brady. "I'm not going to get court orders and search warrants out for every possible Indian in southern Michigan."

Maxon still accompanied Major Brady, however, and when they reached the cabin of Martin and Owaysa, expostulated, "That's where Martin Langdon, the dirty varmint, is livin' in sin with his Injun squaw!"

Martin was watching the approaching column from his corn field at a distance from his buildings. He stopped his husking activities as he saw some soldiers come into his yard.

What he witnessed seemed impossible! Owaysa, being dragged along by two soldiers! He ran faster than he had ever run before in his life.

They had forced open the door — entered his home! His sanctuary! and Owaysa!... Oh, my God, Owaysa!

"What do you think you're doing?" he demanded.

"We're roundin' up Injuns, Langdon!" Maxon grinned.

Martin stepped forward and doubled up his fists. It was no fight, he struck him full on the chin and sent him sprawling across a stump.

"She's my wife, you fools! Take your hands off of her or I'll kill every one of you!" Martin was blind with anger.

"Now you see here!" Major Brady came importantly towards him. "This woman's an Indian. This good man says so." He indicated Maxon. "She goes west with the rest of them. Government orders!"

"Government orders, hell! She's my wife!"

Owaysa, wrenching herself free from the grasp of the soldiers, fell into his arms as she reached Martin's side.

"Can't you see she's about to give birth to a child?" Martin's tone was pleading.

"Orders are orders!" Major Brady said. "I don't run the government. I only do what the government says. Maybe you'd like to go west of the Mississippi too. If you would just keep fighting law and order."

Martin's temper was at such a pitch that he could not refrain from saying, "How'd you like to be cut down to a corporal, Major? I'm sure it can be arranged."

"Threats will get you nowhere! You attacked this good man, unprovoked. You're evidently living with this squaw — "

"Wife! Dammit Since when has a settler's legal wife been forced to go with soldiers?"

"I told you. She's an Indian!"

"Half-breed, sir, if one must be technical." Martin emphasized the sir.

Maxon was reviving and, sitting erect on his stump, he began nursing his jaw and spitting out tobacco juice.

"You ought to be proud of yourself, Maxon! You've done a wonderful job! And now you're trying to get me in trouble, to boot!"

Owaysa was moaning softly, and Brady, hesitating a moment, said to the men, "Better get her a drink of water. She'll be fainting next." The men started for the water.

Martin, taking another tack, said, "Major, you get three dollars a head for every Indian don't you?"

"That's the going price, yes! Above my regular pay!"

"Good!" Martin reached in his jeans and pulled out a leathern pouch. "Here's three dollars in silver! Just leave my wife here and you've made your money easier than taking her across the Mississippi."

Major Brady hesitated only a moment. Then asked, "You sure you really married this half breed girl?"

"In a church in Tecumseh!"

Turning on Maxon the major said, "You told me these people weren't married!"

"Well, I didn't think they was! Lot's of fellers lives with squaws, and—"

"Go on back to your farm, Maxon! I don't need you any more!"

The Major took the proferred money from Martin, and ordered the column to proceed. Old Baw Beese led the procession of Indians, flanked by soldiers. But not even the sad plight of the parting and their heavy guard could prevent their waving good-bye to Martin and Owaysa, as she finally revived and stood dazedly by his side.

Long after the column had gone, and the melancholy chanting of the Indians had died away on the trail to the north, Martin, his own eyes slightly moist, and Owaysa, hers full of tears, and with stifled sobs, went into the cabin.

"It's the end of an era," Martin said. "If it hadn't been for the good Chief Baw Beese almost every settler here would have starved to death at one time or another. But this is the end of a way of life."

They said little more.

And it was that night that Martin David Langdon, junior, was born. Martin had rushed to Sam Pratt's wife for help, praying that Owaysa would survive the ordeal.

*****

SUDDENLY about a week later, Osseo who had not been heard from since his trip put in an appearance at the cabin. He glided sorrowfully into the room, where young David was nestling in the arms of his mother, for Martin and Owaysa had decided to call him by his middle name.

"Been to Ko-jess-sug-wa-seepe!" said Osseo sadly. "Gone! All gone!"

Then he sank down on the floor, and Martin, entering, expressed the hope that he would stay and live with them now that Chief Baw Beese and the others had been moved west.

"No!" said Osseo. "Iowa no good for Injuns! Me go with Chief Baw Beese! Belong with Injuns!"

Martin stepped outside the cabin so Osseo could be alone with Owaysa. He felt that perhaps father and daughter might like to say their final good-bye, alone.

But soon Osseo came out the cabin door.

"I go now—join Baw Beese! Must warn him about west. Bad place for forest people! But some day I come back—see little one—and see town named for me."

Hardly waiting for Martin to say farewell, Osseo rode off up the Kalamazoo trail towards Hillsdale to join the departing band of Indians and Chief Baw Beese.

THE END

Glossary

A-owh — yes.

Ash-te-wette — wife of Baw Beese.

Baw Beese — a main chief of the Huron-Potowatomi, believed to have meant White Swan.

Chee-chee-qua — wife of Sauenquett, meaning robin.

Choo-ween — no.

Cush-a-wees — a minor chief.

Goon-pa-shee — a fortuen teller, whose name means snowbird.

Ke-moke-mon, meaning literally, Long Knife, or American.

Kakatoma — a young minor chief under Moquago.

Ka-moche-kit — a thief.

Ko-jess-sug-wa-seepe — an Indian village named Squawfield by the pioneers.

Me-shup-shee — a panther.

Mick-e-sawbe — the name of an Indian village at Happy Waters, known to the settlers as Coldwater.

Moquago — a main chief of the Huron-Potowatomi at Nottawa seepe.

Nag-doche-shaw — a horse.

Nottawa seepe — the village of Moquago, near modern Athens.

Osseo — meaning song of the evening star. The father of Owaysa.

Owaysa, meaning bluebird, the wife of Martin Langdon.

Pamasaw – son of Chief Baw Beese, and former pupil of Martin, meaning flying bird.

Posho – Potowatomi greeting for hello.

Sau-en-quett – a half-breed minor chief, who ceded Mick-e-sawbe to the United States.

We-no-jah – the Meadowlark, daughter of Moquago.

Pronunciation of Indian words and names is exactly as the spelling indicates. The spellings are phonetic. Where an I is used, it is pronounced as a long I, as in the word *shun-i-ah,* with the accent if any on the *second syllable.* E is pronounced as a long E. In Owaysa, the name is pronounced *O-way-sa*, with the accent on the second syllable.

Notes

THE SCARCITY of authentic data concerning the Indians of south central Michigan necessarily leaves much to conjecture, for the history of the race is recorded meagerly, and entirely by their conquerors.

In many instances the historical facts are the reports of prejudiced pioneers who wanted to occupy the rich lands held by the Huron-Potowatomi, a band who had ceded land to the United States near the Huron and Raisin rivers, before the War of 1812, and had consequently moved westward into what now constitutes chiefly Hillsdale and Branch counties.

The early histories of southern Michigan as written by Crisfield Johnson did not appear until the late 1870s, and were written from tales as told by the pioneers. But these tales in the meantime had grown confused with the stories of wild Indians on the plains, and in no way indicated the culture of the peoples of southern Michigan.

In turning to the Indians themselves one is faced with a folklore that is somewhat inaccurately recounted due to the very regional character of Indians in one locality, who have only imperfect knowledge of those living in another. Perhaps the most confusing characteristic of Indians is the number of separate and individual nations embraced in a territory such as Michigan, Ohio, or Indiana. These peoples, while usually at peace with one another represented several different nations.

In Michigan alone there were actually three or four different and separate nations: The Potowatomi, south of the Grand River; the Ottawa, and the Chippewa or Ojibway, above the Grand River, and the Wyandotte, near Detroit.

In addition to this there were numerous smaller divisions of the same tribe or nation, all of whom claimed a certain autonomy, and violently championed what would be called in a later age the doctrine of state rights.

The right of an individual band to cede land at will was questioned by others, sometimes challenged, but never taken for granted unless the tribal councils had so voted. Chiefs of themselves had little power unless granted to them by the councils. This led to much trouble from the beginning of the white man's dealings with the Indians.

Both the British and French came from countries in which the ruler's word was law. Consequently they both assumed that if an Indian chief signed a document, with or without firewater, it was binding and legal. However, should the council consider the chief's action unwise, the entire document was worthless so far as an agreement was concerned.

Consequently wise chiefs learned as time went on not to sign documents thrust in front of them unless these had first been approved by the councils of their own bands.

The fact that Sau-en-quett deeded Mick-e-sawbe to the United States against the wishes of the combined councils of the assembled Huron-Potowatomi rendered him a criminal in the eyes of the tribes involved. He had defied the edicts of the council.

It is futile to believe that the United States of America did not know in 1838, that the lands had not been ceded as the history books recount at the Treaty of Chicago in 1833.

Therefore, according to Indian stories among the descendants of the Huron-Potowatomi, the government made a final last attempt to induce the Indians to voluntarily go west, and cede their lands. We find no record of this effort in the United States archives, which seems to have been made at Mendon.

There is, however, sufficient local proof of this meeting to justify its incorporation in the early chapters of *Forgotten Yesterdays.*

In the writing of historical novels one is frequently asked for bibliographies, proving the authenticity of the material involved. Such a bibliography was recently compiled by an author who purportedly had made a study of Indians, and while there was little doubt that the source material had been faithfully quoted, the source material itself had mixed Eskimo customs with the practices of the Shawnees.

Consequently I will only say, for those who wish to know some of the sources from which material for *Forgotten Yesterdays* has been drawn have been, first from the living Indians: Levi Pamp-te-pee of the Potowatomi, Chief Wash-suh-kum of the Chippewa. Next, historical data has been gleaned from documents provided by the United States Department of Indian Affairs. Other facts have been gleaned from such books as *A History of the Bean Creek Country* by James J. Hogaboam; Crisfield Johnson's histories of Hillsdale, Branch and Lenawee counties, Michigan; various books on United States history; the Michigan history books of Ferris Lewis; old newspapers, not the least valuable of which have been centennial editions of the *Athens Times* of Athens; and the *Coldwater Reporter* of Coldwater.

Some of the episodes, such as the wedding of Betsey Mergen, are tales from the pioneers. In her instance, the tale was first handled by the famous nineteenth century poet, Will Carleton. The episode of the attempt to tar and feather the land shark with maple sugar was recounted by descendants of the pioneers.

The characters in *Forgotten Yesterdays* are composite in nature, and do not necessarily represent any one particular pioneer. The fact that many pioneers had Indian wives is undisputed today; and there are several cases known where some of the pioneers were themselves Indians, marrying settlers' daughters. Such marriages were by no means the rule, but they did exist in the pioneer era.

Some of the descendants of these inter-racial marriages are proud of their Indian ancestry today, and others do all they possibly can to prevent the discovery of the fact that native American blood flows through their veins, mixed now in only a thin stream indeed with the Caucasian race.

Inter-marriage of races has always been questioned by the ethical standards of all peoples, and probably always will be. But in the case of the two races in America — namely the native Indian and the pioneer, there has been common to them both, a love of individual freedom. But the differences marked between the white man of America and the red man have always been, not so much a matter of color, but cultures that have been completely at odds. The Indian had, and still retains a certain culture of his own — a culture that has not been obliterated since the days the settlements at Jamestown and Plymouth Rock were founded. From this example in history, where the conquerors have all the might of numbers and science, it is easy to understand that the native cultures of peoples can only be eradicated when the race itself becomes extinct.

Greenbrook,
Hillsdale, Michigan.
November, 1963.

MERRITT GREENE